TOPS IN
TROOP 10

TOPS IN
TROOP 10

by *James W. English*

illustrated by
Leonard Shortall

THE MACMILLAN COMPANY
NEW YORK

"Hi Lo, Hi Jolly," "The Thirsty Bass of Dry Gulch,"
"The Straw-Vote Machine," "The Bank Roll Went That-a-Way,"
"The Rainbow Chasers," "Big Toe Rainbow," "The Steam-Heated Hike,"
and "Toby's Ordeal" appeared originally in *Boys' Life*,
published by the Boy Scouts of America.

The Macmillan Company, New York
Collier-Macmillan Canada, Ltd., Toronto, Ontario
Library of Congress catalog card number: 66-11104
Printed in the United States of America
Second Printing, 1967

To George F. Miller, who in nearly forty years
as Scout Executive of the Theodore Roosevelt Council,
Phoenix, Arizona, has kept Scouting an outdoor,
character-building program for all boys

Contents

Hi Lo, Hi Jolly

Did you ever notice that most people want to make history, not study it? Of course, Troop 10's lazy Tailbone Patrol didn't want to make or study history; we just wanted to be left alone.

Ever since we organized the Tailbone Patrol, to protect ourselves against undue work and physical exercise, we had sat on our tailbones while each little crisis passed us by. But even this outfit hadn't a ghost of a chance when history's clear bugle call sounded. From that moment, the Tailboners were trapped by a rush of strange events beyond our control—events which spelled trouble for us in capital letters.

Why, it's trouble enough for me, Mike Peterson, just to be patrol leader of the Tailboners. But let this outfit try to re-create one of history's screwball events of a century ago, and we really did ask for double trouble.

The action took place west of Phoenix on U.S. High-

1

way 70. Back in pioneer days this cacti-studded route to the Pacific coast was called "the trail of graves." Today it is dotted with historical markers, which tell how fate made some rich and failed others who died with their boots on. And it was at one of these innocent historical markers that the Tailboners had our rendezvous with history.

We became involved because Doc, our Scoutmaster, volunteered to have Troop 10 polish, clean, and repair the historical markers along Highway 70. Doc's promise of a Good Turn was the only reason why the Tailbone Patrol was camped under the desert stars and a mesquite tree at a dry campsite beside traffic-jammed Highway 70, some place west of a whistle stop called Quartsite.

We had been hauled in by car, and dumped. We were stranded miles from the closest malted milk, TV screen, or civilized comfort. There weren't any compensations like a nice lake to swim in or a mountain to climb. In this unlikely spot we pitched camp, cooked dinner, then sat around our campfire and griped—an art long since mastered by the Tailbone Patrol.

"You know, fellows," Toby, my overweight assistant PL, confided in a knowing tone of voice, "our noble patrol leader sold us out! Mike drew this dry campsite. But where is the Cougar Patrol? The Cougars are up the road at the *town* of Salome! What do you think of that?"

From their loud yells it was evident the Tailboners

didn't think much of it, so Tommy Thompson kept the ball rolling.

"What a town, that Salome!" he exclaimed. "Why, it has a couple hundred people living there. And where there's a couple hundred people there must be soda pop, juke boxes, hamburgers, people to talk to. . . ."

"Feed our patrol leader to the buzzards!" screamed Beans Roberts.

"Well, boss man!" demanded Toby. "What defense do you plead?"

"Insanity, naturally," I replied. "But don't you guys forget that each patrol is camped by a historical pioneer shrine that they're to repair."

Two-Bits Karsten, our pinch-penny treasurer, challenged me. "And what historical shrine are those undeserving Cougars repairing amid the bright lights of that desert metropolis . . . er, what's its name?"

"Salome!" I added helpfully. "And the Cougars are repairing Dick Wick Hall's 'Laughing Gas Service Station.' "

It took several seconds for this new fact to sink in. Suddenly Beans Roberts demanded, "Who and what was this fellow Hall?"

"Hall was a famous humorist," I replied, having been prodded by Doc, our Scoutmaster, to do a little historical research. "He named the town Salome after the Biblical dancer, because each summer he said the sands around here got so hot they burn your feet and you have to dance. Hall had a pet frog, seven years old, who couldn't swim because he'd never seen water. One of his roadside signs said, 'Smile, you don't have to stay here, but we do.' He died in 1926, and the historical society would like to repair his newspaper office and garage."

"OK. . . . I guess," said Toby. "But what are we going to restore out here, Mike?"

"On the other side of this sand wash there should be a boothill cemetery, and up the road a half-mile farther should be the grave of Hi Jolly."

"That's us, just a bunch of grave diggers," said Toby. "But hey! Who's this Hi Jolly?"

"Just a camel driver," I replied.

"Sure, he's a. . . . He's a what?"

"A camel driver," I shouted above the loud protests of the Tailboners.

"Mike, there are absolutely no camels in Arizona," said Toby. "So what gives with this camel driver?"

"Back before the Civil War, the United States Army was trying to keep supply routes open to the Pacific coast. With the Indians, the deserts, and the lack of water, it was a tough job. So a Lieutenant Edward F. Beale talked the War Department into importing camels for this desert country. That was back in 1856, and nearly a hundred camels were brought into this Arizona territory. . . ."

4

"Hey Toby!" demanded Two-Bits in a hoarse whisper. "Do you think Mike's on the level? Gee whiz, camels!"

I ignored this interruption.

"To drive the camels the War Department brought over Syrian camel drivers. The camels proved much more effective than mules and wagons. But the very sight of the camels panicked horses and mules. The army men couldn't learn to ride the camels. And the camel drivers found life in our west too rough for them, so they went back to Syria—all but one."

"And that one just has to be this character Hi Jolly," said Toby.

"You are so right," I replied. "He was eleven years old when he came to America. His real name was Hadji Ali, but everyone here called him Hi Jolly.

"Now the start of the Civil War," I continued, "ended the camel experiment for good. The camels were turned loose. But Hi Jolly wouldn't desert his camels. He tried to watch out for them here in the desert, where he supported himself by prospecting for gold. For years folks told of suddenly seeing a camel racing across the desert. But, in 1902, Hi Jolly died, and the stories of camels died out shortly afterwards."

Little Billy Spears, our hikemaster, planted himself in front of me. "Mike, you say this Hi Jolly is buried right over there?"

I nodded.

"And the historical society has a plaque at his grave that'll confirm all this camel Hi Jolly stuff?"

"I sure hope so!" I said.

"The plaque had better be there," thundered Billy, "for we're hiking over to see about this Hi Jolly character. Put it in gear, Tailboners!" he shouted. "Let's go!"

It was a short hike, and since there was absolutely nothing else to do, everyone grabbed a flashlight and followed Billy.

Very shortly we were standing before a pyramid-shaped cairn of rocks, topped by a bronze camel. And imbedded in the rocks were bronze plates telling the story of Hi Jolly. The Tailboners crowded around, their flashlights lighting up the plaques.

Toby whistled. "I'll be darned! There were camels out here after all. I apologize, Mike."

"And this guy Hi Jolly was for real!" exclaimed Beans Roberts.

"You know, this history stuff's pretty interesting when you get into it, isn't it?" Tommy Thompson asked.

For a few minutes we sat beside Hi Jolly's monument and watched the stream of cars and trucks with glaring headlights go roaring down the highway. No one gave so much as a toot of the horn or a friendly wave to good old Hi Jolly and his colorful page from history.

"Mike," Beans Roberts asked, "do you know of anyone

besides Hi Jolly who came along this 'trail of graves'?"

"Fortune seekers mostly. Prospectors. Millions of dollars in gold was dug out of these sands during and after the Civil War. The Indians made it dangerous for the miners, and some of those prospectors who didn't find gold in the hills often held up the Wells Fargo stage and robbed it of sacks of gold dust. If bullets didn't get you, and they got plenty, the desert heat and lack of water could knock you off."

Toby, who was still intently watching the cars flash past, sighed with undisguised longing. "Just imagine what would happen," he suggested, "if Hi Jolly and one of his camels decided to stroll down Highway 70 right now."

Two-Bits Karsten laughed. "Wow! The drivers' eyes would pop out; they'd hit the brakes; tires would squeal; cars would bang together. It'd be a beautiful auto-omelet."

Tommy Thompson shook his head. "I wonder if anyone ever stops to read old historical markers."

"Perhaps we should recommend to the historical society that they erect signs, 'Historical museum ahead, admission $1.00,'" suggested Two-Bits. "That'd sure get folks to stop."

As we hiked back to our campsite, Billy Spears summed up the feelings of all of us. "You know," he said, "that guy Hi Jolly was only eleven years old when he came to this country. Then he wouldn't go home to Syria, because he wouldn't leave his camels untended."

"You said it, Billy boy," replied Toby.

"Seeing those folks drive past, not knowing or caring what happened out here a hundred years ago, kind of makes me mad," Billy continued. "I wish there was something we could do to let folks know about Hi Jolly."

There was no doubt that Billy's sentimental wish hit a responsive note, for no one said a thing.

The next morning we cleaned up Boothill Cemetery, but we did our most loving work on Hi Jolly's grave. We patched the pyramid-shaped cairn where stones had fallen out, we polished the bronze plaque, we filled in the gopher holes, we picked up the papers blown over from the highway.

Doc, our Scoutmaster, was waiting at our campsite with more cans of water, additional chow, and some bad news. "The truck is stuck in the sand behind Dick Wick Hall's place in Salome, so we won't be able to haul you fellows and your gear out until morning. But I've brought enough deluxe chow to carry even Toby through until tomorrow.

"The troop will make it up to you, tomorrow," Doc continued. "We've booked a motel at Salome. After showers, you guys can swim all day in the motel pool. And tomorrow night the pioneer society is having us as guests of honor at a real outdoor barbecue."

The ever-hungry Toby let out a yell. "All we can eat, I hope!"

"We getting any publicity out of this Good Turn?" Billy Spears asked.

Doc nodded. "Not quite as I had planned, however," he replied. "The Phoenix papers sent a reporter and photographer who did a little work around Salome this morning. I intended for them to get out to each patrol's worksite, but then the paper radioed them this morning. Seems there was a train wreck near here. The newspaper team and the highway patrol headed for the wreck. But we'll see that everyone gets mentioned. Well, see you in the morning." Then he got in his car and drove off.

"The only thing good I see about this mess is that old Hi Jolly gets the benefit of our company for another evening," Toby said.

After dinner we tossed some more mesquite logs on the fire and were cleaning up camp when Billy Spears came prancing in out of the shadow wearing a weird outfit.

"How do I look?" he asked. "And who am I?"

"Well if you don't know. . . . Hey, fellows, look," laughed Toby.

"He's Hi Jolly! How'd you get that outfit, Billy?"

From an onion sack Billy had cut a headdress, which hung down over his shoulders. A troop neckerchief made a turban, and somebody's striped ground cloth was draped around his waist like a robe. Actually, he wasn't a bad facsimile of what we imagined Hi Jolly would look like.

Just then Toby went "Urk!" The fat one's eyes were about to pop out of his head, and for once Toby was speechless. However, his index finger pointed, gestured, and probed at a spot behind Billy.

"Toby looks like he's seeing a ghost." Beans Robert laughed as he let his eyes follow Toby's index finger. Suddenly Beans said "Urk!" and looked like he'd seen a ghost, too.

Drawn irresistibly like a compass needle to magnetic north, the rest of the Tailboners took a reading along Toby's index finger—and went "Urk!" Our eyes popped, and we were speechless, for there stood a camel.

Billy was the first to regain his voice. "Hey, fellows! I'm me, but who's that thing?"

"We're all accounted for, Billy," I replied. "He's a stranger!"

"Maybe you called for a taxi," suggested Two-Bits.

"Do you suppose there are still some of Hi Jolly's camels around here?" demanded Beans Roberts. "It is a camel, isn't it?"

"I heard on the radio, just before dinner, that some carnival animals were loose after that train wreck near here," Toby said. "Maybe this guy's from the carnival via the train wreck."

"Billy," Two-Bits suggested, "see if our camel's tame enough to catch. There might be a reward for him."

"Our treasurer doesn't mind whose life he endangers so long as there's a buck in it for the Tailboners," complained Billy, but he did move a little closer to our visitor.

The camel bared some dirty teeth and looked at Billy out of cold, unblinking eyes.

"He likes you, Billy," Toby said.

Billy stopped. "Okay, wise guys! So he's my friend. But if I should manage to get hold of him, he'd be Tailbone property. Okay, Mike! Assign jobs to everyone! I'm not the only camel driver in this outfit, am I?"

Under Billy's prodding we closed in, but our visitor didn't show any sign of wanting to run away. In fact, he seemed pleased to have found some human beings.

"Say, Billy, there's a broken rope around his nose. Don't you have some rope we could tie to that piece?" I asked, as I played my flashlight on our visitor's homely face.

Once Billy got the extra rope tied to what looked like a halter rope, we were in business. We led our mount closer to the fire so we could look him over.

"I doubt if he's going to ride like a Cadillac," said Toby, "but if these small foreign camel-compacts were good enough for old Hi Jolly, this model'll do for us now. Right?"

11

"Right!" we answered, for by now there was clearly but one course of action to be taken.

"Think he'll carry all of us?" Beans Roberts asked.

"Camels can carry seven or eight hundred pounds," I said. "Toby's our only hazard, so mount up."

"Find out how to get our mount to kneel down so we can climb on board in style," suggested Tommy Thompson.

Billy, who had been talking to our camel in a friendly,

puppy-dog tone of voice, shrugged his shoulders. But right about then the end of the halter rope swung in against the camel's front legs, and with a grouchy sigh, the beast knelt down.

"Billy, this isn't like hypnosis. You can get him to stand up again, can't you?" I asked.

"How should I know?" Billy replied. "But don't waste time. Get on."

Rather gingerly we climbed on board, holding onto the hump, twining our fingers into the camel's hair.

Suddenly Toby slid off, ran to his duffel, grabbed his uke, and dashed back. He just made it, for Billy had done something which started the camel rising to his feet again. Both Toby and Billy made dives and with helping hands were hauled topside.

Billy sat forward, still clad in the Hi Jolly costume and dangling the halter rope in his hand.

"How do I make this guy go?" he asked. "And if he does go, how does he know which way I want him to go?"

"Quite a minor detail, my boy," pronounced Toby. "You have done admirably so far. We trust you explicitly. Now, boy, steer this desert greyhound to dear old Hi Jolly's monument, if you will. I feel one of my longer speeches coming on."

The thought of one of Toby's speeches brought a unanimous cry of protest from the Tailbone Patrol. And

13

this outcry was apparently just what was needed to accelerate our camel. He lurched forward. So help me that hump wound up—like a pitcher getting ready to release a baseball—and then unwound at twice the speed—and this with every step. Since this critter had four feet, he was taking a lot of steps, and we were suffering effects similar to seasickness.

"Throw me a lifeline, I'm sinking!" yelled Tommy Thompson. I looked around but couldn't see him. "Where are you, Tommy?" I called.

"Some place south of Port Said," he retorted. "Billy! Cut down the revolutions on this thing. He's cracking the whip with those of us on the downwind flight deck."

"Sorry, mates," Billy called. "This model came without a manual of instructions. Just hang on until we reach the first camel service station."

By now the full moon was up, and I noticed that we cast a shadow that looked like an agitated pyramid resting on two pairs of stilts. But at least our new acquaintance was headed toward Hi Jolly's monument. As we approached, Toby started clearing his throat and stood up, holding onto the shoulders of the guy in front.

"Sit down," I commanded. "You're crowding the other passengers."

"Can't help it, Mike. I've got a speech coming on. Just steer this camel right up to Hi Jolly's monument, if you will please, boy." Our camel cruised right on.

14

"Hey! I said to stop in front of Hi Jolly's monument," yelled Toby.

"I don't care what you said," growled Billy Spears. "And this camel doesn't care as much as I do. He's now running this show himself. I can't steer him or stop him."

Now Toby would never let an opportunity for a speech get away from him. "Friend Hi Jolly!" he roared, "despite present unfavorable circumstances, the Tailbone Patrol promises that once more you shall be known to people as the loyal, devoted friend that you were to these desert battleships. And now, for reasons beyond our control, we bid thee farewell."

"Sit down, Senator," I shouted. "There are some telephone wires up ahead, and I think they're lying in wait for you."

"Think we ought to jump off, Mike?" Toby asked.

"Too late," I replied, swinging the beam of my flashlight across the ground. It was covered with cacti.

"Get your flashlights ready, fellows," I said. "I think our ship of state is about to join the traffic on Highway 70. We'll need all the running lights, taillights, and headlights we can get. And just as soon as anyone sees a clear space, bail out."

However, as our lumbering desert water tank approached the highway, he seemed to sense that this modern traffic was moving faster there on the black macadam highway.

"Hey, Billy!" I protested. "I think he's slipped gears and has accelerated."

"Please get your foot off the gas," pleaded Tommy. "I'm seasick."

"I'm sure he means desert sick," said Toby.

"Listen my plump friend, just put yourself between me and the first car that makes camelburgers out of this contraption," I retorted angrily.

"But Mike, this camel wouldn't go up there on the highway, would he?" asked Toby.

"That's right where he's heading," I replied, "and he's going fast enough now that I don't think I want to be a hero at the moment and bail out."

Fortunately, our camel entered our traffic lane at a slight lull between cars. But you should have seen what we did for the traffic approaching on the other side of the road.

And I've news for the pioneer society. The sight of camels not only frightened cattle, horses, mules, and the army privates a hundred years ago; but also automobiles, trucks, and Greyhound buses, today.

A truck driver was the first to pass us. He almost fell right out of the cab of his truck. I was afraid his tractor unit was going to jackknife. When he finally regained control of himself, he slammed down on the air horn and air brakes. This loud noise spurred our camel to greater speed.

By now, cars from the opposite lane were pulled off onto the shoulder of the road in a dizzy pattern of parking, noise, dust, and excited yelling. These people were staring at us as though they knew we were either from Mars or the lockup. And each of them sat on his horn as though he'd just discovered it.

"Fellows, wave those flashlights fore and aft," I screamed. "There's a long line of cars bearing down from the rear."

We started yelling, waving our flashlights, while on the other side of the road horns were tooting, lights blinking, and folks yelling. The confusion was sufficient, the oncoming line of cars slowed down and came to a halt behind us.

By now our charging host had lost his second wind and had slowed down to a walk. Toby dug out his uke. "Maybe I should entertain our audience with 'The Sheik of Araby,' " he suggested.

"Abandon ship!" I roared, giving Toby, uke, and all a shove. "Billy, hold onto the camel's rope," I added.

Our camel was quite docile now, and Billy led him back to the turnoff road for Hi Jolly's monument. We were moving fast.

"Fellows," I suggested, "let's slip back to old Hi Jolly's monument. I don't think there's been such a traffic jam out here since Wells Fargo decided to ship gold dust by stagecoach."

"Yeah! And I see the red blinker light of a highway patrol car trying to get through in this direction," warned Beans Roberts. "Let's disappear."

But that was easier said than done. Once those speeding motorists had stopped, they were curious; they followed us to Hi Jolly's monument. There everyone tried to talk to us at once, and things got all fouled up. I remember one dear lady saying, "I think it is just the cleverest thing I ever heard of. These boys getting publicity for their statue."

Just then a firm hand was laid on my shoulder. "You Mike Peterson?" a husky highway patrolman asked.

I gulped and nodded.

"Good! A pair of lions got loose in that train wreck and are prowling this vicinity. Your Scoutmaster wanted us to bring you guys in. Knowing those killer cats were around is probably why this camel sought your company and let you mount him. We found cat tracks all around your camp. Stay here at the patrol car with the camel while we try to unscramble this mess."

"You know, Mike," Toby said as we watched the patrolmen start traffic moving again, "there sure have been a lot of people seeing old Hi Jolly's monument tonight."

"That's not the half of it, boys," said one of the two men who had joined us at the patrol car. "Every paper in America will carry your picture on the front page tomorrow. You guys were a sight perched on that camel."

I wasn't sure if he was being complimentary or not, but there was something more important at the moment than his opinion of Tailboners.

"If there's a story, you've got to mention Hi Jolly," I said.

"That's right!" the Tailboners yelled.

"He's the reporter," our talkative friend said, indicating the other man. "I'm the photographer."

The Tailboners turned on the reporter. "Hold it, fellows," he pleaded. "I'll get as much about your historical pal, Hi Jolly, into the story as the city desk will allow— fair enough?"

"Hi Jolly deserves every bit of publicity," I said, and the Tailboners agreed.

The Thirsty Bass of
Dry Gulch

Down in the southwestern corner of this country, many habits and customs have been imported from neighboring Mexico. Right here in Phoenix, Arizona, for instance, you can see people wearing colorful Mexican sombreros, or eating fiery south-of-the-border food. But the best custom the Tailbone Patrol adopted from mañanaland is the midday nap, called a siesta.

The trouble with this cultural import was that it overwhelmed us. After the exertion of rediscovering and publicizing that pioneer American, Hi Jolly, the Tailbone Patrol took a mighty long siesta. But while we dozed, less international- and cultural-minded patrols were getting things done. Soon there was no longer any doubt that the Tailbone Patrol was being crowded for top honors in Troop 10.

I decided that henceforth the State Department would have to extend America's cultural relations programs without further help from the Tailboners. Having reached this decision, I threw the psychology stuff out the window. I let the Tailboners have it straight.

"Hey, lamebrains!" I shouted. "Wake up! This patrol has to find a challenge—something that'll put us into orbit again."

Toby vigorously agreed. "Order the patrol treasurer to buy us chocolate malts so we'll have sufficient strength to consider a worthy challenge," he suggested.

Without bothering to open an eye, Two-Bits Karsten shook his head.

"Toby'll want a taxi ride to the soda fountain next," stormed Billy Spears. "But fellas," he pleaded, "Mike's right! This patrol has gotta wake up and do something."

"Like what?" asked Tommy Thompson.

Now, with the Tailbone Patrol you have to be prepared, and I had been waiting for this opportunity. "Like take a rock hound hike!" I proposed.

Such a chorus of howls arose it's a wonder the neighbors didn't call the dog catcher.

"That's a swell idea, Mike," insisted Billy. "We'll go to Wickenburg. . . ."

"But Wickenburg's fifty-five miles away!" said Beans Roberts.

"We'll ride the bus," Billy said patiently. "Then we'll hike to the old mine diggings near the town."

"But we don't know one rock from another," protested Toby.

"It so happens that I have here a few books and pamphlets on the subject," I announced, passing out my literature amidst a chorus of groans. "Now start reading!"

I had forced them into a little action, but the Tailbone Patrol wasn't challenged. They weren't with it, and I was about to ask for a better suggestion when Tommy Thompson suddenly sat upright, semaphoring for attention. "Hey, fellas! Here it is. The challenge Mike wants! And it has Tailbone Patrol written all over it!"

"Cut the TV commercial and get along with the spectacular," said Toby.

"Well," said Tommy, holding up one of the rock hound books. "There's a chapter here on the Wickenburg area, and what do you think?"

"Tell us," muttered Two-Bits.

"There's an old Spanish-Indian legend about the Hassayampa River, which flows right through Wickenburg. According to this legend, whosoever drinks water from the Hassayampa River will never again tell the truth!"

"Come on genius! How does that challenge the always truthful Tailbone Patrol?" demanded Toby.

"That's it!" shouted the exasperated Tommy. "What comes naturally to Boy Scouts? Telling the truth! Right? Well, we'll conduct a scientific test, a noble experiment. The Tailbone Patrol, symbol of the millions of truthful and trustworthy Boy Scouts, will pit our shining Scout heritage and training against the black magic of this old legend."

Toby slipped an arm over Tommy's shoulder. "My

boy!" he said, in a voice filled with respect. "You have a gem of an idea. We'll write the Wickenburg Chamber of Commerce and offer ourselves as guinea pigs in this worthy scientific research. Why, we ought to make the wire services, the picture magazines, the. . . ."

"Remember," interrupted a suspicious Billy Spears, "we're really going rock hunting." But Billy was unheard amidst the general excitement.

Two weeks later we boarded a Greyhound bus in Phoenix. The Wickenburg Chamber of Commerce had accepted our challenge. In their letter they had set a date for the big experiment, and added that they were looking forward to a most entertaining time.

They even added a word of caution, advising that they would resort to any measure, honest or otherwise, to uphold the legendary reputation of the Hassayampa's magic waters.

That last little comment in their letter should have tipped us off to trouble—especially when you consider the character of the town of Wickenburg. It's one of those ghost mining towns that refused to die when the gold diggings petered out. The townsfolk swapped mining picks for boots and saddles and went into the dude ranch business in a big way. The place has more horsy atmosphere than TV westerns. But not all the horseplay is confined to atmosphere, as the Tailbone Patrol was to discover.

Our reception at Wickenburg lived up to even our

fond expectations. The welcoming committee consisted of the chamber of commerce staff, city officials, officials of the dude ranchers' association, and business leaders. And there were plenty of photographers in evidence, too.

"Boy, Mike!" chortled Toby, "we've got the public relations burners cooking."

"But we don't know their angle yet," muttered a still suspicious Billy Spears. "We'd better get our packs and go rock hunting, and pronto. You jerks don't think they're this happy just to see us, do you?"

Fortunately we didn't have to answer Billy since a Mr. Johnson, spokesman for the welcoming committee, was explaining the arrangements. First, they would take us to the Hassayampa River, where we would drink of its legendary waters. Then we would be served a luncheon on the town. By the rules of the contest, we would let the water take effect for one hour before we sought to overcome its legendary evil actions by always telling the truth.

After the contest rules were approved, we were placed in a motor caravan. With horns tooting and folks waving, we sped through town to the banks of the Hassayampa River. Now, the Hassayampa is one of those upside down desert rivers—the water's underground and the bed of sand and rocks is up at the top. The sandy river bed is a hundred yards wide, but the meandering trickle of water needs a road sign to tell it which way to flow.

A bunting draped platform had been erected beside the tiny flow of water. And the place was mobbed. It looked like every dude in the Wickenburg area—and they call themselves the dude ranch capital of the world —had ridden over for the show—meaning us.

"Wow!" I said under my breath. "Maybe we should have taken Billy's suggestion and gone rock hunting."

"Have no fear, Mike. Everything will be all right," Toby said reassuringly. "And this way we latch onto a free lunch. Steaks, I'll bet."

Before I could answer, we were escorted through the mob of horses and dudes to the wooden platform.

"I don't see any gallows. Can't be an old-fashioned necktie party," observed Beans Roberts.

On the platform we were offered chairs, while our official greeters took their places beside us. Mr. Johnson called for attention by striking a metal triangle with a branding iron.

"Hear ye! Hear ye!" he commanded. "Ye medicine men of the Yavapai Apache, and ye brave Spanish Conquistadores. From you noble pioneer spirits we have inherited the treasured legend about our river. Anyone who drinks the waters of the Hassayampa River will never again tell the truth.

"Now, brave pioneer spirits, your legend is being

challenged. These Boy Scouts—the Tailbone Patrol they call themselves—state that they can drink of the Hassayampa's waters; and, because Boy Scouts are pledged to be truthful, these Boy Scouts claim they can continue to tell the truth.

"To make certain that they have drunk sufficiently of the Hassayampa's mystic waters, and the waters have had time to take their dire effect, these courageous but foolish Scouts agree to wait one hour after drinking the waters before starting the contest. Then, if caught in an untruth before leaving town, we will brand these Tailboners with a "laughing H" brand, indicating that forever more they are slaves to the strange powers of the Hassayampa—powers known to your Indian and Spanish forerunners of this wonderful land."

Someone sounded a hoarse blast on an old cowhorn.

A cowboy, a galvanized bucket in hand, strode down to the Hassayampa, where he ladled a pailful of water. He set the bucket on the table in front of us, while someone else produced eight glasses. Billy Spears muttered something about needing to boil the water, but I growled at him that it was safe to drink since it came from underground.

"Do you members of the Tailbone Patrol of the Boy Scouts of America have any last minute requests before starting on this dangerous test?" Mr. Johnson asked.

We were in this scheme much too deep to soft pedal

26

things now, so I stood up and raised my hands for silence.

"As Patrol Leader of the Tailbone Patrol, Troop 10, Phoenix, Arizona, I speak for these and for all Boy Scouts. Is this the most untruthful water you have?" I sat down amidst a roar of laughter from the assembled dudes.

"The very same!" said Mr. Johnson as he ladled out full glasses for each of us.

Every Tailboner drained his glass of Hassayampa River water to the last drop, smacked his lips, and asked for more. The assembled dudes cheered loudly and long, and it was evident they were giving moral support to the underdogs. But it was also apparent to each Tailboner that our courteous hosts had something up their sleeves other than their elbows. And this worried us.

As we rode back into town in the cars, followed by a noisy crowd of dudes on horseback, I had the sickening feeling that we were going to get the ax anyway this show worked out—and that everybody knew it except us.

Yet, the luncheon was a fine affair. Toby had been right; small T-bone steaks especially named Tailbone specials were on the menu. Everyone was friendly. As Toby said, "Mike, everyone's so kind I'm getting kinda nervous."

From where we were seated, we could see a big clock

on the wall, and every Tailboner kept his eye on that
minute hand as the contest time approached.

The conversation by our hosts was becoming a question of who could tell the biggest whopper, and some of
their yarns were utterly fantastic. Every stretching of
the truth was blamed upon the Hassayampa River water.
And after each yarn, someone would ask if we could

top that yarn, since we had just drunk from the Hassa-yampa. Patiently, we always declined.

Then, when only five minutes were left on the clock before the contest started, Mr. Johnson asked me a direct question.

"Mike," he said, "in your letter you stated the Tailbone Patrol was coming to Wickenburg to do a little rock hound prospecting?"

I nodded agreement.

"This confuses me," Mr. Johnson stated. "I never before heard of rock hounds using a glass spinning rod and reel. And you do have such a rod and reel sticking out of one of your patrol's packsacks."

I nodded. "Toby, my assistant, is the champion fly caster in our troop. He usually brings along his rod and reel and practices wherever we go."

Mr. Johnson turned his attention to my assistant. "Surely you don't expect to catch anything in our dry gulch, do you, Toby?" he asked.

"Come on Toby. Give us a fish story," our hosts begged.

Toby got to his feet, looked carefully at the clock to be certain time remained for his yarn, and then plowed in.

"First, let me thank you for that Tailbone steak. It was delicious. Now let me tell you about something just as delicious, which apparently you gentlemen have completely overlooked. I refer to your famous dry gulch bass. It is true that there is not sufficient water on top of the ground for the bass, but how about the great underground flow of the river?"

Mr. Johnson jumped onto this whopper faster than a district attorney on new evidence. "How do you catch these dry gulch bass?"

"Oh," replied Toby, his eyes on the last remaining seconds on the clock. "It takes a much more experienced fisherman to catch thirsty dry gulch bass than a normal wet kinda bass."

"And you can catch them?" insisted Mr. Johnson.

"Natch!" said Toby, sitting down just as the clock reached the contest starting time.

As though by prearranged signal, our hosts roared with laughter.

"Scouts," said Mr. Johnson, "you should never trust such sneaky cowpokes as me and my friends. We were out to trip you, for our legend is very dear to us. So we had the hands on that clock set back ten minutes. Therefore, all of Toby's yarn was on contest time. Now, either you produce your thirsty dry gulch bass out of the Hassayampa River before you leave town, or we'll proclaim the superiority of the Hassayampa over the most truthful efforts of the Tailbone Patrol and the Boy Scouts of America."

He waited a minute for this bit of information to sink

in, then asked, "Are you ready to concede now, fellows?"

I stood up, although my underpinnings were shaking. "Having checked my own watch, I concur in the underhanded trick played with the time piece here," I said. "Now, I'm not at all sure that we should thank you for the lunch, but I am sure we'll do our best to get those dry gulch bass here by this time tomorrow."

Our hosts applauded, congratulated us on our sense of humor and spunk, and said they were looking forward to a wonderful time.

A more shamefaced, downhearted group of Tailboners you've never seen.

"You guys should string me up to the tallest cottonwood tree," wailed Toby as we walked off.

"We were all taken in," I retorted. "I knew something was being pulled on us, but wasn't smart enough to know what it was."

"So now all we gotta do is get some bass out of the dry old Hassayampa," said Beans Roberts.

Without much enthusiasm we shouldered our packs and started hiking down Main Street to the river. I guess everyone in town knew about our goof, the way we'd been trapped. Everyone, but everyone, from toddlers to grandpas, wanted to know how to catch dry gulch bass.

"Us and our big public relations deal," Tommy

Thompson growled. "When this yarn goes out on the wire services, every Boy Scout in America will be out to get us."

"You see, you guys should have listened to me and gone rock hunting," said Billy Spears, smugly.

I guess we'd been waiting for this. We hadn't been able to fight back against the entire town's population. But Billy was no match for the rest of the patrol. After a brief scuffle we were all resting on various parts of his anatomy while discussing things.

"Mike, old boss man," Toby said, "what sort of strategy do you propose to follow if we are to catch these elusive dry gulch bass, which my blabber mouth invented, just ten minutes too late in the day?"

"Yah, Mike! You're PL, and we sure need leadership now," added Tommy Thompson. "A whole new species of bass we gotta find by noon tomorrow. Wow!"

From beneath the crush of Tailboners, Billy grunted. "If you loco brains would get off, I might have a sensible suggestion."

"What? Go on a rock hound hike?" Beans laughed.

"Maybe we should have listened to our eager little hiker," commented Toby. "It would have saved me putting my feet in my mouth."

"Our mouths!" corrected Billy. "And if you guys will just park the dead weight someplace besides on my backsides, I'll put my computer brain to work."

"Let's hear what he has to say," I suggested. "Billy couldn't upset our plans—we don't have any."

"If it wasn't for the reputation of the Boy Scouts of America, I wouldn't be doing this," muttered Billy as he struggled to his feet.

"Such loyalty may get you smothered next time," I warned. "Now, out with it, Billy-boy. What's this hopeful bit of information you have for your suffering patrol?"

"What was the name of that game warden we worked with here, a year or so ago?" he asked. "Remember! The whole troop came up when we read about a flash cloudburst washing out the quail right at nesting time. We packed grain all over these hills for that guy, and lugged in hundreds of stranded baby quail before snakes and hawks got to 'em."

"Yeah!" I replied. "What was his name? Lawson. Yes! Jim Lawson."

"But what does that have to do with helping us find bass where there aren't any?" Toby demanded.

"I was coming to that," shouted Billy.

"Now, when the troop finished that Good Turn, Jim Lawson said to call on him if he could ever do us a favor, didn't he?"

"That's right," I replied. "And at least that's a more sensible starting point than any of you other lamebrains have come up with."

"But, Mike, I'm not through," protested Billy.

He hesitated, then turned to me. "Mike, I think the two of us better have a secret strategy meeting," he said. "Because if what I think is true, is true, these maniacs would be sending up smoke signals for reporters for something I'm not sure is going to come off."

"This brainstorm had better not be as mixed up as that sentence," I warned, as I led him out of earshot of the other Tailboners.

After listening to Billy I called Two-Bits. "Open the patrol vault and give the lad a buck. He has patrol business to perform."

For once Two-Bits was sufficiently awed by the occasion to cough up the money without a squawk. And, with the dollar safely in his pocket, Billy went to town.

"Don't you think he might need some help?" inquired Toby.

"He's not so small he can't blow a dollar on his own," said Two-Bits.

"Fellows," I said, "let's start our dinner. And save some for Billy. It's just possible he may be able to get us out of this jam."

We had finished eating when Billy returned.

"Well, when do we see Jim Lawson?" demanded Toby. "And what can he do for us?"

"We don't see him," Billy said. "Our friends are afraid to be seen talking to us. The welcoming committee is building a corral in the middle of town, where they expect to brand us tomorrow noon, before plenty of photographers and reporters and townsfolk."

"Wow!" wailed Toby. "What'll we do now?"

But I had caught the glint of a smile in Billy's eyes, and knew his telephone conversation had produced results.

"First thing you can do is loan Billy your fishing equipment," I said. "The rest of you guys dig for worms. And Billy, I'd like to have a few words with you while you finish eating."

By the time the fellows got back with a can full of worms, it was dark. I handed over Toby's fishing equipment, and Billy shouldered his pack, picked up his breakfast groceries, and started hiking up the Hassayampa River away from the curious eyes of townsfolks.

"What's the pitch, Mike?" the Tailboners demanded. "Give before we use you for a rocking chair."

"You guys let one peep of this out and Jim Lawson's name is mud in Wickenburg," I warned—then continued. "Well, when the rest of us were sitting around on our tailbones after our Good Turn Quail Rescue last year, Billy was poking his nose around in back of Lawson's barn. And he found two big metal containers filled with bass fingerlings from the state fish hatchery. Lawson told Billy he was going to run a little private experiment, planting the fingerlings in some caved-in mine diggings along the Hassayampa flooded by the river's underground water flow."

"Billy's done it!" shouted Toby happily.

"We'll know tomorrow around noon," I replied. "Billy will spend tonight by one of the ponds so he'll get an early start fishing. Now hit the sack. Tomorrow may be a wonderful day."

Next day, just before noon, Billy hove into sight carrying a string of ten of the most beautiful bass you've ever seen. The Tailbone Patrol, packed and waiting, swung in behind him and started a most triumphal march right up Main Street, Wickenburg. In front of the branding corral (and were they ready for us), we presented the string of thirsty dry gulch bass to Mr. Johnson, who, along with his committee, was too surprised to know what to do. But we knew. We flagged down a Phoenix-bound Greyhound bus and got out of town.

"You know," Toby observed as the bus crossed the bridge over the Hassayampa, "if we'd planned this windup a little better, I bet we could have gotten plenty of pictures and some national publicity."

The rear seat in the Greyhound bus was a bit uncomfortable on the way home, but we didn't mind. As long as we sat on top of Toby he didn't have much opportunity to talk about big public relations deals.

The Straw-Vote Machine

The old saying "The bigger they are, the harder they fall" is no square talk. Brother, it's authentic! The Tailbone Patrol will vouch for that.

After being all but run out of Wickenburg, we had to buckle down to some Scout advancement work just to retain our self-respect. Soon we were again riding high, wide, and cocky as top patrol in Troop 10, and bending everyone's ear with our self-admiring small talk. And then we took our fall.

It started one night at a troop meeting. Doc announced that Troop 10 was expected to participate in the Boy Scouts' nationwide Get Out the Vote campaign for the coming national election. I should have taken my cue from Doc, but I didn't. I just wasn't with this one, nor were the other Tailboners, and we talked most of the troop into our way of thinking.

"Aw, Doc!" wailed Toby, who at all times is alert to

37

the possible danger of being trapped into physical exercise. "You mean we gotta see that everyone in our voting precincts gets one of these Get Out the Vote reminders to hang in his window—or if no one's home, we hang it on the front doorknob?"

Doc nodded. "It's really quite simple unless you're allergic to work."

"But Phoenix is a growing city," Toby pointed out, not catching Doc's sarcasm. "There might be a couple thousand more doorknobs by next week."

"Yeah!" complained Tommy Thompson. "And hundreds of new dogs, who'll forget they're man's best friend and try to ventilate the seat of your pants."

That's when Foxy Walker, PL of our nearest rivals, the Cougar Patrol, sounded off. "Doc," he said sarcastically, "it's obvious that this good turn presents insurmountable obstacles to our genius patrol, the Tailboners."

"Listen, Foxy," I snapped back, "if folks want to vote, they'll get to the voting places without us to remind them."

Foxy didn't say much else, for his entire patrol was siding with us. In fact, the whole troop was. But Doc cut us off curtly with the announcement that there would be a Patrol Leader's meeting after troop dismissal.

That meeting was short but far from sweet. Doc told us to imagine what this country might be like today if folks hadn't voted in years past. "We need to get all Americans to vote," he said. And then he clobbered us —me in particular. "If some wise guys here think slipping Get Out the Vote door hangers on doorknobs is dull stuff, it's because they're too thick-headed to make something worthwhile out of this good turn. They're lazy, physically, mentally, and morally lazy."

With that, he stormed out of the Patrol Leader's meeting.

"Wow!" exclaimed Foxy Walker. "Doc sort of put it on us PL's to do something original with this good turn, didn't he?"

"Foxy," I replied dutifully, "for once you're making sense. I'd say the status quo on this good turn had better be fractured by next troop meeting, or some heads, meaning ours, are going to get cracked."

"Listen, Mike," he pleaded, "let's share any good ideas we get. It'll be for the good of the troop, and this isn't going to be an easy work project to sell to our patrols."

"I'll share this much with you right now," I replied. "Call this good turn a work project, and every Tailboner will be limping along on asthmatic cylinders. We hate work!"

After leaving Foxy, I stopped by the Palmcroft Drugstore, where, naturally, I found the Tailbone Patrol at work on chocolate sodas.

"Hey, Fritz," Toby called to the German boy who's

soda jerk on the night shift. "Mix up some gooey stuff for Mike. He looks kinda down at the mouth."

Tommy Thompson, who'd been giving me the silent once-over, spoke up. "Okay, Mike. Let's have it! What happened?"

"Fellows," I said, "the Get Out the Vote campaign is on."

The uproar was so violent that Fritz fumbled a scoop of ice cream in midair.

"This is a democratic patrol, Mike!" Two-Bits Karsten howled. "We haven't voted!"

"That's right!" yelled Toby, who momentarily forgot his ice cream.

So I told them how things were, and their faces got glummer by the minute. "And here's a lot of literature on the project," I added, tossing some papers on the counter.

The guys groaned.

Fritz placed the retreaded ice cream soda in front of me.

"Mike," he said, "tell these lazy braggarts what Doc means. They'll be protecting their American heritage."

"How come, Fritz?" several of us demanded.

"You guys know I wasn't born in the U.S.A.," Fritz said, "but I have my first papers and now I am studying for my citizenship examination. It's a wonderful country!"

"Sure," interrupted Toby, "but why should we walk our legs off to get folks to vote? That's their business isn't it?"

Fritz shook his head. "All through history man has fought against harsh and unjust rule, against repressive kings and dictators, because man cherished the opportunity to govern himself. This struggle of the common man has existed since ancient times. It split the Greek city-states, and was even voiced in the Roman Empire. Our present word 'veto,' which in Latin means 'I forbid,' was shouted in the Roman Senate to protest dictatorial actions. And man's most recent violent struggle to protect his freedom was against a dictator named Hitler.

"Since recorded time, man has fought to earn the right to vote. The United States has fought wars both to win and to protect that right. And you guys don't think it proper for you to encourage people to get out and vote!"

The Tailbone Patrol at long last understood the problem. Even Toby. He picked up the campaign literature, which I had dropped on the counter. "I'm taking this stuff home with me, Mike," he said. "Got to put my brain to work and see if we can't eliminate the exercise from this good turn."

Next afternoon a sad bunch of Tailboners gathered at my house. Of course, I was more sympathetic than sad, for the doctor had just cut an ingrown nail from my

41

big toe, and I had orders to keep off my foot for several days.

"Honest, fellows!" I apologized. "This wasn't deliberate!"

"Why didn't you have him put a splint around your neck?" demanded Billy Spears.

"Fellow Tailboners," called out Toby, who was putting in sack time on the sofa, "I think we can utilize Mike's extremely limited abilities. You see, I've figured out this good turn. There's no need to slip a door hanger on a single door or hike a single step."

"No doubt we've a genius in our midst," I said.

"Genius is seldom appreciated," observed Toby smugly.

"Okay," I grumbled, curious about his idea in spite of myself. "What's most on your mind?"

"The comfortable life, Mike. Good food, lots of rest, a place to ease the tired body."

"Never mind how you got into the awful shape you're in," said Two-Bits impatiently. "What's this miracle plan of yours?"

"Publicity!" purred Toby. "Publicity for the straw-vote machine. Now, this morning as I sat in the Palmcroft Drugstore and ate an ice cream sundae. . . ."

"Before breakfast?" snorted Beans Roberts.

"Between breakfasts," corrected Toby. "Well, I got to thinking about our good friend Fritz getting his citizenship papers next month. Did you know he's studying pre-med at the college in the daytime? Or that some of the doctors at the Palmcroft Medical Center are making a project out of Fritz? They're going to put him through medical school."

"Okay, society reporter," I said. "How'd you dig up the info, and what's it mean to us?"

Toby looked at me and laughed. "Sure that hangnail wasn't between the ears, Mike?

"Well, as I was saying," he added, turning his attention back to the Tailboners when I couldn't think up a quick answer, "Mr. Colton, proprietor of the Palmcroft Drugstore, told me this information, and in turn I told him of our problem. You see, I had figured out how he and Fritz and the business and professional men at the Palmcroft Shopping Center could help us. Mr. Colton liked my idea so much he's getting all these important people together tonight. Maybe he'll have a few others, too, like the judge who'll grant Fritz his citizenship, the city election commissioner, and a newspaper editor.

"And I'm rather proud of this next step," he added. "It was really psychic on my part—a realization that our PL would chicken out—so I invited them over here, Mike, tonight at eight P.M."

"You what?" I yelled.

"Never mind that," interrupted Tommy Thompson. "Let's find out what it's all about."

The Tailbone Patrol dragged our Assistant PL off the sofa, and after some roughhouse got the entire idea from him. And you had to hand it to Toby. This was a lulu, and it would really make the troop's other patrols look silly.

"We'll need an attorney to check city ordinances," I said. "I'd better call dad."

44

Beans Roberts was next on the telephone. "Pop's an electrician and this is some wiring job."

"My uncle is something or other in the carpenter's union," spoke up Billy. "I'll bet he'll help."

That afternoon we ran up a telephone bill that bankrupted the Tailbone Patrol's treasury, but even Two-Bits was too excited to complain. And that evening our house was so filled with visitors that it looked like the nominating convention of one of the national parties. When the confab broke up, you'd have thought we had George Washington and Abraham Lincoln as running mates on our ticket, everyone was so enthusiastic.

Next day dad cleared all the necessary red tape with the city. The newspaper editor promised to break the story on page one on Wednesday evening, which is troop meeting night. And Mr. Colton, representing the trades and professions at the Palmcroft Shopping Center, promised that a full-page announcement ad would be ready for Wednesday's newspaper.

A few more calls, placed by Beans Roberts' father and Billy Spears' uncle, assured us of donated lumber, loudspeakers, PA system, banners, and all the carpenters and electricians needed to complete the job.

If, in those few happy days before the story broke, the Tailboners looked like the cat that'd swallowed the canary, just mark it down to ignorance, complete ignorance of the power of modern publicity.

I had my first misgivings as I read the story and ad in the Wednesday evening newspaper. Boy, we had the publicity. You see, the trades and professions at the Palmcroft Shopping Center were sponsoring a Get Out the Vote booth in their parking lot. The labor unions had erected the booth, and a PA system was piped into each store. We had a stack of patriotic records, donated by a radio station. We'd taped a little speech by Fritz about what it meant to him to become an American citizen. The election commissioner had a plea for everyone to vote, and the judge handling Fritz's citizenship stated that just before election, Fritz would be sworn in as an American citizen in our booth. And, boy, the Tailbone Patrol was mentioned all over the place, even our names, and that was what started me wondering if we weren't riding a ring-tailed comet on a nonscheduled flight.

The telephone started ringing. Folks congratulating us, folks wanting more information, folks saying they'd be over to sign our pledge books, folks out of our election precincts saying they'd be over anyway.

I left my mother taking down telephone messages and slipped out to troop meeting.

First person I ran into was Foxy Walker, with a copy of the evening paper, and he was really mad.

"Thought you were going to share any bright ideas!" he snorted. "Instead of hogging all the glory for the Tailboners."

"If *I* had any bright ideas," I corrected. "This one was Toby's. Besides, you didn't report any brilliant strategy to me."

He turned away, and I knew then that all he'd been able to come up with was the door-to-door canvass idea.

Well, if Foxy had been cooled off by what he read in the paper, the rest of the troop would have made the Antarctic seem like a friendly jungle paradise.

I gathered the Tailboners around me. "Fellows," I said, "we've stirred up trouble. The phone's been ringing at the house ever since the newspapers hit the street."

"Ditto," muttered Toby and the others. "We need a switchboard."

"Brainchild!" I replied, facing my fat assistant. "I've a feeling this patrol is going to need a whole lot more than a switchboard. The troop's frosted at us, thinks it's a publicity grab, and the way those calls are coming in, I think we'll need all of the troop and then some to operate that booth."

Everyone looked at Toby, who for once was too nervous to take it easy.

"Look, fellows!" he pleaded. "I just think up these wonderful ideas. It's up to you guys to make 'em work."

Fortunately for the health of our Assistant PL, Doc called troop meeting at that moment. When we sat down after the Pledge of Allegiance, I noted that there were enough copies of the evening paper in evidence to start a couple of newsstands. Doc had one in his hands.

"I see by the newspaper that one patrol has its Get Out the Vote campaign in high gear. Mike, tell us what gives!"

"It's very simple," I said. "The publicity and the PA system bring people over to the booth, where they sign the roster for their election precincts. They pledge themselves to vote and we give 'em their Get Out the Vote hangers. The precinct books are listed by streets, and we check the street numbers against the city directory to see if we have everyone. Those we miss at the booth we visit and give 'em doorhangers and a sales talk. We're out for 100 per cent voting in our precincts."

"It's a swell idea," Doc said, "but I'm wondering how you're going to have enough hangers to give to everyone who comes to the booth, since you expect folks from all over the city."

This problem I hadn't counted on. I got red in the face and turned to Toby. "Give, brain, I need details."

"And I'm wondering, too," Doc added, "how you're going to keep the booth open all day for three weeks and still stay in school?"

The troop started to laugh.

"Oh, I wouldn't laugh," Doc cautioned. "The Tailboners are the only patrol who have done anything about this good turn. What they've done is tops. The only problem is they seem not to have thought out their problem very thoroughly."

48

"That," I said under my breath to my squirming assistant, "is the understatement of the year."

"But, Mike," Toby whispered back, "all those adults backing us aren't dopes. Someone must have thought of these problems."

That stopped me, for he was right. Now dad, for instance, has a legal mind that doesn't let a lot of loopholes spoil a project. But if he'd thought of these problems, why hadn't he told me about them?

"Doc," I said, "the Tailbone Patrol would like a recess to make a telephone call."

I talked to dad on the telephone for some time, and when I hung up, I knew less than before I placed the call. "Fellows," I said, "I got the snow job from my own dad. All he'd say is that the Tailbone Patrol has made such a reputation for carrying out our wacky ideas that he and the other men never questioned our capabilities. He said we've bragged about our great abilities so often that he is convinced."

Two-Bits waved a calloused fist under Toby's nose. "Come clean, lamebrain, who suggested this idea to you?"

"It was mostly mine," he said meekly. "Mr. Colton just added a few points."

"Who started the conversation? You or Mr. Colton?" I demanded.

"Well, he asked why I was so down in the dumps,

and I told him about the Get Out the Vote campaign and he told me about Fritz, and the first thing you knew we had a project."

"If a guy comes by wanting to sell the Brooklyn Bridge, keep your hand out of your pocket," I snapped. "You were taken, and took the rest of us with you."

"But why us?" Toby demanded.

"Well," I added, "I seem to get the drift that some folks think we've been spouting off a little too much about being top patrol. Doc made a reference to it; dad certainly said as much. Even Foxy Walker wanted to share ideas, and Foxy isn't the type. Before this, even when we were in trouble with the troop, they'd speak to us. Tonight it's the silent treatment. We've had it."

"Well, let's go back and face the music," Tommy Thompson said. "Only, I wish I could tune in the troop."

Doc gave us a curious look as we came back in and sat down.

"What's the report?" he asked.

"No report," I replied. "The Titanic went down, and so might the Tailbone Patrol."

Foxy Walker was on his feet pronto. "You Tailboners better not flub this one. Not after all that publicity. All the rest of the troop would get a bad name, too."

Doc stopped other uncomplimentary remarks. "I'll call the Scout office tomorrow and see if you can have more Get Out the Vote hangers," he said. "Afraid you'll have to work the other problems out for yourselves."

Saturday morning it was a very nervous group of Tailboners who officially opened our Get Out the Vote booth. If a Tailboner has ever been humble, we were humble at that point. We were scared, too.

In the first half-hour we handled over one hundred persons who stopped at the booth to pledge themselves to vote. Then the deluge started. Folks came in cars, they came lugging squirming kids, they parked bundles of groceries in our arms while they signed, they gave us doctor's prescriptions to run to the drugstore with while they stood in line. To tell you the truth, we ran ourselves ragged.

Toby, completely out of training for such physical exertion, was dripping wet. His Scout shirt looked like Monday's wash.

"Mike," he gasped, "who said this would beat peddling the hangers from door-to-door?"

"You, brain," I replied, as I juggled two oversized sacks of groceries someone had parked in my arms. "And the day's hardly begun."

"Oh, you Tailboners haven't started to see the crowd yet," enthused an elderly gentleman next in line. "Why, that publicity downtown is the best I've ever seen."

"Publicity! Downtown?" I asked.

"Why, yes," the gentleman replied. "There are Scouts

51

on every street corner with sandwich signs. You should read those signs!" For a moment his eyebrows knitted together as he tried to recall one. "Here's one. 'You've learned about the Tailbone Patrol's Vote Booth.' Then the next fellow's sign reads: 'In the newspapers or on the radio.' 'Well, we're the lamebrains who didn't think up that nifty idea.' 'But we're lazy too and don't like to hike all over town.' 'So please hike out to their booth and save us blistered feet!' "

He laughed at the recollection. "They paraded down the street just like those funny shaving cream signs you pass on the highway, and folks all stopped to read what was coming next."

"That sounds like Foxy Walker and the Cougar Patrol getting even," Toby muttered.

A woman behind the gentleman shook her head. "Oh, nearly every troop in town is represented," she said cheerfully. "My son belongs to Troop 32, and his patrol worked the last two nights getting their signboards in order."

Beans Roberts, who had just arrived on the scene, grabbed the packages from my arms as I sank into a chair.

"What's the matter, Mike?" he asked. "You look like you need first aid."

"I do," I replied. "A tourniquet around my neck."

Just then Billy Spears dumped a canteen of water on me.

"Break it up, you politicians," he roared. "We haven't time for any heart attacks now. Look at our customers. One of you brains had better give before the police riot squad arrives."

I looked up and did a double, then a triple, take. The entire parking lot was jammed with folks. It looked like the mob trying to get out of the stadium after a football game. Only, we were the exit, and we were most definitely a bottleneck.

Hurriedly, I rounded up some cardboard and painted on the precinct numbers. We tacked these signs up, and then we circulated around, getting people in the proper lines. It was still a madhouse, but some of the confusion was missing. All we needed was about four times as many Scouts; then we could have done a first-rate job.

I leaned against a side of the booth, trying to get up enough strength to check on the lines of people pledging themselves to vote.

Doc arrived about that time. He was smiling.

"Doc," I said, "we're snowed under."

"And we've been sabotaged," Toby replied. "All the troops in Phoenix are planning to get our records and see who in their precincts haven't pledged to vote. The lazy dogs!"

"That's the way you fellows asked for it," Doc reminded us. "You made this a Tailbone activity, not a troop or council affair."

"So we goofed," admitted Toby. "And when we

goof, we don't do it in any minor, piddling fashion. We really goof."

"We owe you and the troop an apology," I told Doc. "Not a little apology, but a great big one. Guess we have a lot to learn about democratic processes, bending the will to the majority vote, playing it for the good of everyone instead of our own special gain."

"We should apologize to the entire council as well as the troop," Beans Roberts added. "How stupid can one patrol get?"

Doc grinned and waved to someone beyond the crowd. In a couple of minutes the rest of Troop 10 was on hand.

"I figured that four hours of this would cause the Tailbone Patrol to see the light," he added. "You fellows take a short break at the drugstore. Fritz has malts and hamburgers waiting. Troop 10 will take over the vote booth."

We were halfway through our lunch when Doc joined us.

"Tell me, Doc," I asked. "Who really thought up this idea?"

Doc laughed. "Mr. Colton and I had worked it out as a troop project and cleared it with the council office. I'd planned to introduce it at troop meeting, until you guys poured cold water on the whole good turn. Then Mr. Colton and I decided to wait and see if anyone who came along asking for help would be foolish enough to run with the idea alone."

"Then all those adults at that meeting knew the whole troop would participate after we got bogged down?" Toby asked in amazement.

Doc nodded. "You might say that the only really original idea was Foxy Walker's sandwich sign gag, which all the troops in Phoenix went for in a big way.

"Oh, yes," he added, "you fellows might like to know that the mothers' clubs of the council's troops are each taking the booth one day a week until the Scouts of Troop 10 get out of school. The troop will have the duty from 3 P.M. until closing time week days and all day on Saturdays. Okay?"

"It's wonderful, Doc," I said, and the Tailboners were yelling so loud that poor Fritz missed another scoop of ice cream in midair. But then, he didn't seem to mind. Why should he? He understood the meaning of democratic action all along.

The Bank Roll Went
That-a-Way

Nothing excites the red blood corpuscles of an Arizona native quite as much as the Eastern visitor who expects the West to be a carbon copy of the cowboy thrillers on TV. All that Troop 10's Tailbone Patrol needed was Boston-bred Johnathan Reardon III. This kid would have been disappointed at a *Gunsmoke* TV filming if they'd been using live bullets. Johnathan wanted real pioneer Western action, he said. The Tailbone Patrol vowed we'd give him that action—but how?

"If we knew any Indians and had some tea, we might stage another Boston Tea Party," suggested Toby.

"Is this the way a gunslinger walks?" asked Tommy Thompson as he strutted past, twirling an imaginary six-shooter.

"Naw!" said Two-Bits Karsten, our cynical treasurer, "just waddle the fat man's waddle, like Toby."

"But Toby couldn't be a gunslinger," protested Beans

56

Roberts. "On TV, gunslingers are skinny guys. Less target to shoot at, I guess."

This gives you a small idea of our problem. So we called on Doc, Troop 10's Scoutmaster and indirectly the cause of our trouble. Johnathan was his house guest, being some distant relative.

"Doc," I said, "this Bostonian thinks we've tucked away all the Western badmen just to spoil his visit to Phoenix. Now, we'd like to shoot-it-up for him, but Doc, we don't know how to be Western badmen. What'll we do?"

Doc grinned. "Sounds like an impossible assignment even for the Tailbone Patrol." But after a moment's thought, he added, "Maybe a historical hike would convince Johnathan that Arizona wasn't always civilized."

"A what kind of hike?" asked Billy Spears, our hikemaster. You could see the thought made him happy.

"I mean for the Tailbone Patrol to take Johnathan some place where exciting early pioneer action took place," Doc said. "Fill him in on the history; show him where it happened. Back where Johnathan hails from there are Revolutionary War sites everywhere, and folks from out here visit those historic sites all the time."

"Sounds reasonable," I said, "if we only knew of a historic site around here."

"I got it!" shouted Beans Roberts. "We'll go to Maricopa Wells!"

"Maricopa what and where?" asked Billy Spears.

"I went with my grandmother to the Arizona Pioneer Society's picnic the other night," Beans said, "and heard about this Maricopa Wells. It was a change-over station for fresh horses on the Butterfield Stage route. It's in Telegraph Pass where the Gila River cuts between the Estrella and South Mountains. Even in pioneer times it was so isolated down there that the U.S. Cavalry was always rounding up marauding Indian bands, stage robbers, swindlers, and gamblers."

"What's it like today?" Toby asked.

"Pretty much forgotten, I guess," Beans said. "The remount station was burned down a couple times. Has a boothill cemetery where they buried them with their boots on. And supposedly there's $10,000 of Wells Fargo gold hidden nearby. Stage robbers hijacked a gold shipment, but a cavalry unit at Maricopa Wells closed in so fast the robbers buried the gold and tried to shoot it out with the troops. None of the stage robbers survived, so no one knows where the gold was buried."

"We'll take along shovels and treasure maps!" shouted Billy.

In no time at all it was evident that the Tailbone Patrol was going to take a historic hike.

Doc promised to check on the campsite and drive us down, as Telegraph Pass is a forgotten bit of earth southwest of Phoenix with not even a good road nearby.

Doc's information indicated we'd selected a real historic site all right, but would be making a dry camp. So we loaded Doc's station wagon with two ten-gallon milk cans filled with water; but Tommy Thompson and Toby insisted on bringing along an empty third milk can. "In case one of the others springs a leak," Toby said.

Doc shook his head. "I'm not asking questions, but from the weight of Toby's pack and this empty milk can, I'd say you've got some horseplay on tap, Mike. Better watch these two conspirators."

The road to our historic site skirted the Maricopa Indian Reservation and the tip of South Mountains. But once we left the farmlands and headed into Telegraph Pass, the going was rough. What passed for a road was a little-used wagon track across the paloverde-, mesquite- and cacti-studded outwash slopes of the South Mountains. And there wasn't any sign of life for miles around, except for numerous coveys of quail.

Soon the road reached the banks of the broad and sandy Gila River. Our side of the river was desolate and hilly, while on the opposite bank the steep slopes of the Estrella Mountains plunged right into the riverbed.

"Golly," grumbled Toby, "I bet there isn't a hamburger stand within thirty miles."

But Johnathan was pleased. "This is more like it!" he said. "But it is peculiar that I've never heard of this Maricopa Wells on any of the TV programs."

"The pioneers here were all too busy being pioneers to sign up for TV shows," said Two-Bits.

"See that high ridge ahead?" Doc asked, pointing to where the trailing slopes of the South Mountains met the banks of the Gila River. "I believe that's our spot. The stagecoach station was placed there because attackers could only come from two sides, which made it easier to defend."

"But why did we bring along drinking water, if there's a well there?" asked Johnathan.

"It's been nearly a hundred years since the stagecoaches bounced through this pass," Doc said. "The well has long since caved in, and if there is any water in the river, it's not fit to drink."

The road climbed the steep ridge, wound through some smoke trees, and came out on level, open ground. In the center of the clearing were some crumbling adobe walls, which once had surrounded the stagecoach station and horse corrals. Beyond the walls was the boothill cemetery and, judging by the number of graves, there once was enough action at Maricopa Wells to have satisfied even Johnathan.

As it was, Johnathan hiked around the old stagecoach site while we unloaded and made camp beneath a lone cottonwood tree growing inside the walled enclosure— probably at the spot where the well had been located. When Johnathan came back, he was as excited as a kid with a candy bar. He'd found old wagon wheels and a tin cup with a hole through it—which he was sure was a bullet hole.

Doc ate lunch with us and then headed back to Phoenix.

Toby stretched out comfortably under the cotton-wood tree, tuned in some jazz on his transistor radio, and started eating a candy bar.

"You history hounds can search around," he said. "I'm taking my siesta."

Johnathan was appalled. "Here we are, where stage-coaches raced bandits and Indians—where the U.S. Cavalry fought to keep the stage route open—and you want to sleep. Why, I'm so excited, I probably won't sleep a wink tonight."

"That," Toby said with a sly wink, "may be the understatement of the year!"

Recalling the empty milk can, Toby's extra-heavy pack, and Doc's warning about conspirators, I had an uneasy feeling. "If you intend to sack out, fat boy," I said, "you are hereby appointed chef for tonight's chow. And Tommy, you'd better come with the hikers," I added, intent on keeping these two conspirators separated.

"Where we going, Mike?" Tommy asked.

"That's Billy's department," I replied, pointing to our hikemaster, who already looked like an army-surplus display rack. He was carrying a canteen, a trenching shovel, a map of the area, a compass, and gosh knows what all he had stuffed in his pockets.

"Are we digging or hiking?" I asked.

"Maybe both, Mike," Billy replied enthusiastically. "According to the historical records, the last time this pioneer bus station was burned out, the occupants made a run for it to the south. Indians and renegades hemmed them in, and they put up a last-ditch fight on a rocky point just a couple miles from here. The description of this point, jutting out into the Gila River, sounds like the same place where the Cavalry put an end to the bandits who robbed the stagecoach of that Wells Fargo gold. Thought we'd hike down there and take a look-see. Maybe we'll find the buried gold."

"I'll send for an armored truck," Toby said.

As we hiked down the old stagecoach road, I pulled Tommy Thompson aside. "What goes with you and Toby?" I demanded. "And what's the empty milk can for?"

"Tonight we're going to give Johnathan a little Western excitement," Tommy replied. "Nothing for you to get fired up over, Mike."

"Maybe not," I muttered, "but it sounds like a dirty trick to play on a visitor."

"You know, Mike," Tommy replied, "the more Johnathan tells me about the old West, the more I'm convinced not all pioneers played by the Marquis of Queensberry rules."

"I'll talk to you guys later," I said. "Right now it looks like Billy's found the old battlesite."

Where the stagecoach station at Maricopa Wells had been cleaned out of most souvenirs, the battlesite proved a veritable historic gold mine. We found the rusted barrel of a rifle, a broken knife blade, several horses' bits, and some other odds and ends.

Our Eastern dude was elated. This was pay dirt. Now he had historical facts that hadn't as yet appeared on TV. But Two-Bits wasn't satisfied.

"This patrol needs that lost Wells Fargo gold," he kept reminding whoever was holding the trenching shovel. "You gotta dig! Dig! Dig!" But all of our digging accomplished nothing.

The sun was already hidden behind the Estrella Mountains when we started back to Maricopa Wells. It was the lateness of the hour, I think, that surprised us when a light plane came zooming through the pass. And then in a few minutes the plane returned, skimming as low over the terrain as the pilot dared.

"How can the old West escape modern civilization, when you've got hot-rod airplane pilots, like that?" said Two-Bits.

"I'm glad I'm not up there," I replied. "That plane was darn low, and there's sure no place around here for a plane to make an emergency landing."

When we got back to Maricopa Wells, we found Toby with his ear glued to his radio. Dinner had not been started.

"This," announced Two-Bits, "is unbelievable. When he's the cook, Toby usually prepares the meal so far in advance that he's eaten half of it before the rest of the patrol arrives."

"Listen, wiseguys!" Toby shouted, "we may be in for some real excitement. Late this afternoon a couple guys held up the bank at Buckeye and got away with $12,000. The police think they're headed this way, right through Telegraph Pass."

"How come?" I asked. "Wouldn't this be off the beat as an escape route?"

Toby shook his head. "Police found their stolen getaway car abandoned in brush beside the Salt River, just above its junction with the Gila. The police theory is that the robbers crossed the river on foot and were picked up on this side by a companion in another car. Police had that plane flying through the pass trying to spot this second car and get a description of it.

"The belief now is that the plane will keep the car holed up out of sight until dark, which gives the police time to establish a roadblock on the Phoenix side. The law thinks the robbers will try to sneak through Telegraph Pass into the Casa Grande Valley after dark. And if that's the case, do you jokers realize who the modern counterpart of the U.S. Cavalry is going to be? It'll be up to us poor little Tailboners to do or die at historic old Maricopa Wells." Toby finally stopped for a breath.

Johnathan, who had been listening intently, smiled and shook his head. "A very good try, Toby, but you just don't understand the format of true Western action. You'll have to frighten me with a better yarn than that!"

"Yeah," I said, "is this part of your conspiracy to frighten our Boston expert on the West?"

Toby angrily turned up the volume on his radio. On station after station there was nothing but special bulletins about the Buckeye bank robbery.

"But Doc knows we're in danger! He'll come get us, won't he?" inquired Johnathan a little anxiously.

"If the law's throwing up a roadblock on the Phoenix exit, they won't let Doc through," I replied. "He'll have to convince the police we're likely hostage prospects, so they'll send some deputies in to wet-nurse us. But the question will be, who gets here first—the bandits or the deputies?"

"How soon can the police put a roadblock at the south end of this pass and bottle us up with these lovely characters?" asked Two-Bits.

I turned to Toby for an answer.

"Seems this is such a little-used road," he replied, "and the Casa Grande Valley has so many prospector's trails crossing the desert that the law isn't sure of the route. There've been a couple of pleas for guides who know the way in here from the south."

"Billy," I said to our hikemaster, "break out your map of this area."

The map showed Buckeye about twenty crow-fly miles north of us, just above the junction of the Salt and Gila rivers. To the south, Telegraph Pass emptied into the broad Casa Grande Valley, where the bandits could cover an awful lot of miles by a number of back roads through the desert.

I looked at my watch and realized there would be complete darkness in another half-hour. "Fellows," I said, "I think we'd better vacate these premises and seek a more secluded motel site. Billy, fill canteens and be prepared to take us up the South Mountains by some route where we won't be conspicuous.

"And the rest of you—minimum packs. Toby, pass out what chow we can eat cold. And get a move on!"

I noticed Johnathan hung onto his relics of the old West. "Mike," he said, breathing heavily, "this is just like the old Wells Fargo holdup. Confidentially I really didn't expect the modern West to be so exciting!"

We were ready to go when Toby pulled me aside.

"Mike," he said, "maybe we could take the stuff Tommy and I intended to frighten Johnathan with and fix a little surprise for the robbers. That is, if we leave some gear in sight and they come over to investigate."

"What's your plan?" I demanded. "And make it quick! I don't want to be the newest addition in that boothill cemetery."

Toby explained his plan and, for him, it was a most rational idea.

"Billy," I said to our hikemaster, "lead the patrol up that draw you've selected as our escape route. Toby, Tommy, and I will join you in a few minutes. Now get going!"

In a few minutes we too were on our way, but it was completely dark when we reached the other Tailboners —perhaps a mile from Maricopa Wells and several hundred feet higher.

"Any moon tonight?" I asked.

"Not till about eleven o'clock."

"Say, what were you three guys up to?" Beans Roberts demanded.

"Not much," I replied. "We just dragged some of our equipment out in the open where the robbers would be sure to see it."

"You did!" exclaimed Johnathan. "But why? The robbers will know we're nearby."

"If I read you guys correctly," said Billy Spears, "you aren't content just to play it safe. You think we can help capture the bank robbers. Hey, look!"

The blinking wing lights of the small plane were coming toward us, and in a minute we could hear the roar of the engine. The plane flew through the pass, and then returned shortly.

"Quiet!" demanded Billy Spears. "I think I hear a car."

"I don't see any lights," said Tommy Thompson.

"If it's the robbers, they'll try driving in the dark—especially with that plane flying overhead," I pointed out.

"Hey! I hear the car now," exclaimed Johnathan. "What if it's the robbers and they see our camping gear you guys left out in the open? What do you think they'll do?"

"Yeah!" said Two-Bits. "We who are about to die would like to know the grand strategy."

"Listen!" I said.

Now you could clearly hear the car creeping up a steep grade, the tires crunching over the loose gravel.

"They must be crossing this draw and climbing the hill to the stagecoach station," Toby muttered.

"They'll stop if they see our gear," I replied. "Then in a few minutes we'll know!"

"Know what?" demanded Billy. "This is no time to be playing guessing games."

"You tell 'em, Toby," I said.

"Well," he said, "Tommy and I came prepared to give Johnathan a fright tonight. Besides the empty milk can, we brought along some special gear."

"That's why Toby's pack was so heavy," Tommy added.

"Wait a minute!" I interrupted. "I think their car has stopped."

Everyone was quiet, but we couldn't hear a sound.

"What do you think is happening?" asked Johnathan.

"I know what I hope is happening," muttered Toby.

Suddenly the silence was shattered by a deafening roar. It sounded like a giant Fourth of July fireworks blast, only this sound didn't die out. It swelled to ear-splitting proportions and then bounced off the rocky walls of Telegraph Pass until it echoed like a dozen explosions.

The Tailboners and Johnathan hit the dirt and wiggled behind outcroppings of rock like veteran front-line combat troops. All, that is, except Toby, Tommy, and me. The three of us were jumping up and down, slapping each other on the back, and shouting like the madmen we were.

It was Billy who recovered first and tackled me. "Listen, Mike," he pleaded, "I know Uncle Sam didn't give you guys an atom bomb to test-fire just so you could frighten Johnathan. Now what was that explosion?"

"Wait a minute," I said. "There's a second part to this, and it should be happening any second now."

"Yeah," added Tommy Thompson, "we think those robbers may be so surprised and frightened they'll do something kinda nutty."

For a minute everyone peered into the darkness. Below us someone yelled, car lights flashed on, and a car suddenly hurtled off to the south at breakneck speed.

"Look!" shouted Johnathan. To the north three sets of car lights snapped on and, with red blinker lights flashing, sped in our direction. Overhead the tiny plane zoomed, circled, and headed south toward the fleeing car.

"Wow!" muttered Beans Roberts. "Your explosion sure frightened the robbers into revealing their position. And now the law's hot on their trail."

"That plane will stick to them like a bloodhound," I added.

"Boy! Look at that," exclaimed Two-Bits. To the south, in the flat desert of the Casa Grande Valley, half a dozen car lights snapped on. Guided by radio messages from the light plane, the cars raced to head off the flee-ing robbers.

"Fellows," I said, "if anyone thought to bring flash-lights along, we can start hiking back to our historic pioneer site. Our interlude with modern adventure seems just about over."

Johnathan fell in step beside me.

"Mike, what was that explosion? What had Toby planned for me?"

"Yeah! How do you make a boom like that with a milk can?" demanded Two-Bits.

"Well," Toby said, "I borrowed a miniature cannon from the high-school R.O.T.C."

"The one they use to fire 12-gauge shot gun blanks

71

when they have parades and reviews," added Tommy.

"And you pointed the muzzle of the cannon into the mouth of that empty milk can?" asked Billy.

"That's right," Toby replied. "Figured it'd make a bigger noise."

"But how did you trigger it? How'd you make it go off just when you wanted it to?" demanded Johnathan.

"That's where the packs left out in the open come in," Toby explained. "We attached some fishline to the firing mechanism of the cannon and then tied the fishline to the packs. Anyone lifting up those packs, or tripping over the line between the packs, fired the cannon."

"And you guys were going to do all that just to show me some real excitement?" demanded Johnathan.

"The Tailbone Patrol aims to please," I stated. "And if it's action out West you want. . . ."

I didn't finish, for I could hear Doc calling us. "Here we are!" I shouted. "We're coming in!"

A squad car was parked in front of the stagecoach station, motor running, as a police driver monitored radio reports from the plane and the police cars closing in on the fleeing car.

"Caught the robbers yet?" I asked.

"It'll be just a few minutes now, thanks to that booby trap you Scouts set. You'll find your Scoutmaster over there with the sheriff," and he pointed toward our camp.

Doc, the sheriff, and several of his men were inspecting our cannon-milk-can contraption.

The sheriff greeted us warmly. "Any time you Scouts want to join the force, let me know. Fact is, think I'll appoint all you fellows special deputies when we get back to Phoenix."

"Wow!" yelled Johnathan. "A sheriff's badge. Wow!"

"They caught 'em!" shouted the police driver. "They gave up without a fight. Tried to hide the money first, but the pilot spotted the location, and the money was recovered."

"Well, I'm glad it's over, fellows," Doc said. "And I'm proud of you Tailboners. How about you, Johnathan?"

"I'm putting them right up with the U.S. Cavalry, the Vigilantes, the Texas Rangers, and all my other heroes of the West," he replied. "This was some action!"

And for once, Johnathan knew what he was talking about.

The Rainbow Chasers

Out here in Arizona we have a considerable history of losing gold mines, which carelessness naturally led to the sport of finding lost gold mines. This get-rich-quick sport dates back to the year 1540, when a Spanish grandee, Francisco Vasquez de Coronado, toured the southwest in search of the fabled seven golden cities of Cibola.

Coronado didn't find a single pot of gold, but this hasn't dampened the dreams of other rainbow chasers. Annually, thousands fall to the lure of lost gold, including those perennial paupers of Troop 10, Phoenix—the Tailbone Patrol.

We were meeting at my house when the gold bug bit us. We were suffering through the dreary financial report of our dour-toned treasurer when Toby rudely interrupted him.

"Two-Bits," he said, "you should leave a little cash in

the till instead of blowing it all. Then we wouldn't have to bail out your inadequate bank balances."

"Yeah! Yeah!" chorused a suddenly expectant Tailbone Patrol.

"You guys voted to spend every dime," roared Two-Bits. "And if our Assistant P.L. would put a girth hitch around his appetite, we might even have a modest bank balance."

"Mike!" complained Toby, ignoring the patrol's laughter, "this spendthrift's passing the blame for our being broke on me. Do something!"

"Knock it off!" I growled. "I'm appointing Toby a one-man committee to come up with a plan by next week for ending our financial troubles."

Toby arrived at our next patrol meeting with an armful of aerial photo maps, photostats from the newspaper morgue, penciled notes, and a satisfied grin.

"Okay, friend Midas," I said. "Tell us of your golden touch."

"Yeah!" demanded Two-Bits. "I don't know what Mike said, but let's see you fill the patrol treasury with riches."

"I was only instructed to decide how to fill our treasury with rocks from Fort Knox. And I have that answer," shouted Toby. "We'll find the Lost Dutchman Gold Mine!"

I can't describe the howls of outrage at this announcement, so let me tell about this most famous of lost gold mines.

Now, gold mines get lost because there is a lack of brotherly love when gold is involved. When the Spaniards found a mine, the Indians used the Spaniards for archery practice, after which the Indians obliterated signs of the gold diggings. Years later, if the Indians didn't dispose of the prospector, bandits did by using the gold miner for a pistol target. Naturally, such friendly neighbors prevented anyone from admitting he knew the location of a gold mine.

Now, the Lost Dutchman Gold Mine is somewhere in the Superstition Mountain Wilderness Area east of Phoenix. As the story goes, a Dutchman named Jacob Waltz surprised three Mexican boys working a lost Spanish mine. Waltz shot the Mexicans and worked the diggings himself.

The Dutchman was a free spender of his gold nuggets, and many not-too-honest types tried to follow him to his mine. It's a matter of newspaper record that these chaps were found with bullet holes in their heads.

Jacob Waltz died in Phoenix in 1884, without revealing the mine's location. Since then, prospectors, professional and amateur, have searched for the Lost Dutchman Gold Mine, and their luck has been uniformly bad. And some never came back.

"But if old Jacob Waltz didn't tell anyone where his private version of Fort Knox is located," I demanded of

Toby, "how do we know where to look for his gold mine?"

"Right here!" Toby said, pointing to a grease-pencil line drawn across an aerial photo map of the southeast quadrant of the Superstition Mountains. "Some records discovered in Spain gave a clue to the location of a gold mine in the Superstitions. Landmarks described in the Spanish papers are identifiable today—the Gila River and Picket Post Peak. The distance traveled and the compass bearings from these landmarks tell us the Spaniards entered the Superstition by way of Peralta Canyon. They hiked up-canyon to a point described as 'beneath a towering pinnacle, believed to be what we call Weaver's Needle,' so. . . ."

"Wow! Clear to the top of the Superstitions," exclaimed Beans Roberts.

"A mile high and four thousand feet above the desert floor—where we'll start our hike," announced Billy Spears.

Toby nodded. "I, who find hiking distasteful, shall make personal sacrifices that the Tailbone Patrol may become Scouting's first patrol of millionaires."

"La-de-da! Listen to the man!" Beans Roberts laughed.

"You guys know a nutty banker or someone who's going to pay for our transportation and food now, before we've found our gold mine?" asked Two-Bits.

I grinned. "Our practical Tailbone treasurer suggests

we each negotiate a thirty-day loan from our parents, secured by our solemn pledge of cash repayment or extra work on the home premises."

Beans Roberts moaned, "Boy, we'd better find the Dutchman's gold."

One morning soon afterward, the Tailbone Patrol started hiking up Peralta Canyon in the rugged Superstitions. Since leaving the bus and highway nearly two hours earlier, we had seen no human beings. However, in this lower portion of Peralta Canyon a trail led through the cacti, greasewood, and mesquite.

"Looks like the weekend curiosity seekers come this way," muttered Beans Roberts as he observed the litter.

"They're nuts!" grumbled Two-Bits, glancing up at the somber, towering cliffs and precariously balanced rocks. In places where rocks had fallen, we had to scramble over the debris. After one such stretch of rough going, Billy pointed out that we no longer had a weekend hikers' trail—we were moving into the vastness of the Superstitions, into that wild region beyond the exploration of the merely curious.

We ate lunch beside a huge boulder on the floor of the canyon, and the sands beside the boulder were moist and damp.

"Should be a seepage spring farther up," our alert hikemaster pointed out.

"Until we find fresh water, go easy on your canteens," I cautioned. "We might not find a spring by nightfall."

"How about finding the Dutchman's gold?" said Tommy Thompson.

As we shouldered our packs, Beans Roberts looked at the gloomy cliffs overhead. "Let's not camp in this canyon tonight," he said. "This place gives me the creeps. No wonder folks say it's haunted!"

Such a comment, admitting to a slight case of nerves, usually brings down a storm of Tailbone derision. But not this time. Instead, we hiked in moody silence, a novel experience in the life of the Tailbone Patrol.

"What happened to the Spaniards who found this gold mine?" I asked Toby, suddenly anxious to talk to someone.

"Don't really know," Toby answered. "It's believed that Apache Indians ambushed them in this canyon, killing the entire party—including Pima Indians the Spaniards had helping them. You know, the Pimas still won't enter the Superstitions. Claim ghosts haunt these peaks."

Instinctively we glanced at the battlement walls.

"The Spaniards sent several search parties, but the Apaches had destroyed all signs of the mine. It remained lost until found by the Mexicans whom the Dutchman shot."

We suddenly bumped into the other members of the Tailbone Patrol, who stood silent, intent, listening.

"What's the matter?" I asked in a hoarse whisper.

"Listen. Right behind the wind," said Billy quietly.

Then we heard—Toby and I. The sound was unmistakably the metallic clang of a small bell. Then the bell fell silent; only the lonely sound of the wind remained.

To the unspoken question "What is it?" I shook my head. I glanced at my watch. We could hike on for another half-hour and still get out of the canyon before dark.

"Let's get going," I said finally. "Billy and I will lead. Spread out between hikers. Toby'll bring up the rear. Let's go!"

We pushed ahead, through dense smoke trees and greasewood, only to emerge on a barren spot beside a pool of smelly water. Beside the pool stood a dead sycamore tree, its bark peeling off. To a branch was fastened a cowbell. Strong gusts of wind caused the branch to sway, the bell to rattle.

Billy laughed outright. A sense of relief swept over us. But Beans Roberts pointed out some disquieting facts.

"Guess that cowbell didn't put itself up in that tree," he said.

"What's it there for?" Tommy Thompson asked.

"Probably a warning sign beside a poisoned water hole," Beans said. "Lots of small animal skeletons in the underbrush here."

A quick glance confirmed this bleak observation.

"Certainly the water was fresh when that tree was

growing," Beans continued. "But something killed the tree and those small animals. Maybe the bell is meant to frighten away larger animals, deer, members of the cat family, wild pigs."

"Come on!" I said without enthusiasm. "Let's get hiking."

If we didn't get started, I was afraid I'd lose my nerve; only I didn't know what I was afraid of.

"You think that water was poisoned by someone?" Billy asked as we hiked on.

"Looks like it," I replied, wanting to change the subject before he asked why and who. Then I noticed the clouds overhead. The fleecy cumulus clouds of morning had piled up into towering black thunderheads.

I pointed to the sky.

Billy nodded. "We're going to get wet," he said in a flat, listless tone.

Then he stopped, and pointed to some bleached bones across the wash. They were the nearly decomposed remains of two deer.

"Probably drank from that poisoned pool!" Billy said.

Suddenly he pointed to the dust. Unmistakably there was a footprint of someone wearing hobnailed boots. We were not alone in Peralta Canyon.

The other Tailboners crowded around.

"That footprint was made today," Beans Roberts pointed out. "What do you make of it, Mike?"

I shrugged. "It's a free country. No law says only Tailboners can come up here. Let's go!"

We hiked on, but the feeling of impending disaster was so strong it frightened me.

"Whoever made that footprint plans to spend the night up here, too," observed Billy.

We were scrambling through a jumbled rock slide along the canyon floor, when we heard the shot.

Billy and I searched each other's faces with quick oblique glances—looking for clues of reassurance.

I tried to rise to the occasion. "Hard to tell what caliber gun—canyon walls distort the sound. Perhaps our friend just shot his dinner, a rabbit or quail."

I slipped out of my pack. "Keep the other fellows low, behind these rocks. I'm going to scout ahead."

I slipped between two tilted boulders and was suddenly alone; alone in an empty wilderness that was no longer empty. Who was up ahead? What kind of man? And now, the legends of the Superstitions, the stories—whether fact or fiction mattered not—populated my mind with visions of murder, lust, revenge.

By my watch I had been on my own for fifteen minutes, when I peeked over the edge of a canted boulder and saw my quarry.

He was a burly man, booted, bearded, of rough exterior appearance, intently and deftly at work with a large hunting knife. He was working beneath some cottonwood trees, and between us was a large pool of clear blue water.

Now I knew what had happened. This man had lain in these rocks, just as I was doing, and had shot a deer as the animal drank from the pool. He had killed the deer out of season and was now cutting the choice sections from his kill.

And then an even more ominous thought entered my

mind. No doubt this poacher had poisoned the water hole down stream and tied the cowbell to the tree. He wanted to keep the deer by this pool, so it would be easier for him to kill his meat supply. But why was he living in the canyon? Why? Why else—the Lost Dutchman Gold Mine. Instinctively I knew this sort of man, a law unto himself, would not look kindly on anyone else entering his domain in search of the lost gold he probably felt was rightfully his.

With an empty sickness in the pit of my stomach, I knew why, over the centuries, the loss of life in the Superstitions was so high.

I did not want to move until I saw where the man would go. But I was afraid the Tailboners, worried by my long absence, would look for me and inadvertently reveal our presence.

When I reached the Tailbone Patrol, I explained our situation.

"What shall we do, Mike?" Toby asked.

"We can't get out of this canyon tonight," I said. "But, if our friend goes on up-canyon, I'd like to fill our canteens and start back. . . ."

"Okay! This place gives me the willies," said Tommy Thompson.

The others nodded.

"We can only do what this hermit prospector's movements allow," I pointed out. "And we'd better find out what he's doing. Toby, keep the patrol quiet and out of sight. I'll take Billy with me—so we can send back a message. Good luck!"

As Billy and I approached the boulder, which overhung the pool of sweet water, we inched over the weatherslick rock on our bellies. When we peeked over, our man was gone. I was certain he was not hiding. With the bold confidence of one who prefers a lonely self-sufficiency, he would be off to his permanent campsite. But where was that campsite?

I motioned for Billy to stay where he was, and, dropping between two boulders, made my way out to the pool. Along the water's edge I saw where the deer had been drinking when shot. The man had dragged the deer to the cottonwood trees, where he had cut off the hind quarters. Then he dragged the carcass through the brush. I followed and found where he had left the carcass for the vultures—I also found a clear trail of hobnail footprints leading up the canyon.

Billy could see me now. Using my arms, I semaphored for him to get the canteens. Beans Roberts returned with Billy. I put a halazone tablet in each canteen to be sure of the water's purity. Then the three of us started back.

A bright flash, a blinding streak of lightning, which illuminated our gloom-shrouded canyon, momentarily startled us. The lightning faded into deeper darkness as an earsplitting crash of thunder shook the very canyon walls.

"Wow!" muttered Beans Roberts.

I looked at those splintered canyon walls and the boulder-strewn canyon floor and too late knew why the hermit-prospector's campsite was not by the pool of water we'd just left. Something in those canyon walls, probably a metallic deposit, attracted lightning. This was why these cliffs were splintered and the canyon floor was littered by rock slides.

"Listen!" Billy whispered.

With a rush of wind, like the sound of a waterfall, a sheet of rain swept over the canyon wall and engulfed us. Flashes of lightning showed us the way, for with the rain had come the deep and total darkness of a storm-racked night.

When we reached Toby, he had the patrol crouched under an overhanging boulder.

"That first bolt of lightning gave us a rock shower," he said. "I think we should get out of here."

For an hour we sloshed through rivulets of water as it rushed off the canyon walls. We were drenched, cold, and dispirited.

When we reached the open canyon floor, by the poisoned pool, what had been a dry stream bed was now a good sized flood of rising waters.

A series of lightning bolts slammed into the walls, up-canyon where we had been. The ground literally trembled, and we could hear above the roar of thunder the rending of rocks from the canyon sides. The rock slides had started.

"Boy, that lightning was so close you could hear it sizzle!" exclaimed Tommy Thompson.

"I think I saw the mouth of a cave where this shale slope meets the cliff," I said. "Let's try it."

We labored up the slippery stones toward a black opening. It extended back a good ten feet, but at its highest point was only four feet high. The cave's dusty floor was almost a continuation of the steep slope we had climbed. However, we were out of the rain and beyond reach of the wind. And this part of the canyon wall had, through the centuries, been no magnet for lightning.

"No wonder the Pima Indians think evil spirits live in the Superstitions," muttered Two-Bits. "And they're right!" he added.

"You know," Billy said, "I've decided to hate those Spaniards for finding this gold mine in the first place. Look at the trouble it's caused ever since."

"Yeah, but how did the Spaniards haul enough gold out of this Apache stronghold to make it profitable to operate the mine?" asked Beans Roberts.

"This vein was almost pure gold," Toby replied. "They'd bring in a pack train of supplies, cache some where the Apaches wouldn't get it, and dig their gold— perhaps forty or fifty men. Others took the horses to one of the Pima Indian villages until time to return."

"What'd they cache?" Two-Bits asked.

"I suppose pack saddles, horse trappings, mining tools, maybe an arrastra or two. . . ."

"A what or two?" Beans asked.

"An arrastra, a flat stone used for crushing ore into fine particles—easier to transport."

"Where'd they hide that stuff so the Apaches couldn't get it?" I asked.

"I suppose in a . . . a cave," Toby replied.

"Who's got a flashlight?" Beans asked. "Something's sticking me in the back."

Billy passed a light to Beans.

Suddenly, the hikemaster let out a strange gurgling sound and drew back. Beans Roberts cleared his throat. "Don't let me spoil an otherwise charming evening," he said, "but there's a skeleton beneath me—I think it's a human skeleton."

"The head was poking Beans in the back," Billy said in a squeaky voice.

There was no mistake about it. They had partly unearthed a human skull.

"Oh, great!" moaned Two-Bits. "Just the bed I've always wanted for a stormy night."

"Play that light over here," I said. "Let's see what other cheerful discoveries we can make."

Before long even we knew our cave was a historic storehouse. Several bridle fastenings and pieces of metal horse trappings were found. Also a large round smooth stone we couldn't dig out, which Toby thought was an arrastra. There were some hand-cut nails, a crumpled

Indian storage basket once filled with corn, another skeleton, plus several arrowheads.

"Looks like the Apaches found this hiding place," Toby said.

"You think these guys were Spaniards, and this stuff theirs?" Two-Bits asked.

Toby nodded.

With the first rays of the morning sun, we hiked out of Peralta Canyon. We were a grimy, tired, empty-handed bunch of gold seekers, although Toby carried some of our cave discoveries for souvenirs.

We managed to hail a bus at the highway and reached Phoenix. Toby called the state historical museum, and his mother delivered our discoveries while we slept.

We awoke to find museum staff, TV cameramen, and newspaper reporters looking for Tailboners.

"We're in demand, Mike," panted Toby when he reached me by telephone. "What'll we do?"

"We're being grub-staked by the museum to lead their crew to our cave. The state game department's sending a couple of officers along with a John Doe warrant for the arrest of our canyon neighbor. And Two-Bits just called with a tremendous money-making scheme. . . ."

"I don't want to hear it!" shouted Toby.

But if you had driven to the foot of Peralta Canyon during the next month—while the cave was being dug out (it did have Spanish relics in it)—you'd have seen our Tailbone gold mine.

Just as Two-Bits had anticipated, all that publicity brought throngs of the curious to the mouth of Peralta Canyon. And there we had our store. Our sign read: "Tailbone Explorer's Club—soft drinks, hot dogs, candy for sale—information on our historic discovery freely given."

True, we didn't find the Dutchman's Lost Gold Mine, but we created a different sort of gold mine. Two-Bits now has a healthy cash balance in our Tailbone treasury, and we are living it up at the Palmcroft Drug Store while planning our next expedition.

Which proves that when you're rainbow chasing, or when you're a Tailboner, the gold you bring home may not be the gold you expected to find.

Big Toe Rainbow

Ever since a British chap named Izaak Walton wrote about skipping work to go fishing, he-men have claimed the art of angling for their own. The Tailbone Patrol was no exception, for at the close of school we left the desert heat of Phoenix for the mountain coolness of the Scout council's Camp Geronimo.

It had been a good year for the Tailboners. Each of us had our share of spinning reels, glass rods, fancy flies, and oversized creels, and we were itching to try them out in Tonto Creek, a nifty trout stream.

However, wherever you have Tailboners you have goofs. And let me tell you, this was a major goof. It happened at campfire the night before trout season opened. Now anybody in Troop 10 would tell you that the Tailbone Patrol just naturally tells big fish stories. But that evening we set out to tell the biggest fish story ever heard at Camp Geronimo. Maybe it was the blazing campfire, the wind in the pines, or the thought of using our new fishing gear the next day. Not only did we make bluegills sound like muskies, but were so carried away with the story of our fishing skills that we promised to land the biggest trout caught this year from Tonto Creek.

Next morning, in the cold light of a new trout season, neither aspirin nor vitamin pills could shake our chills. The awful realities of our bragging had at last clobbered us—trout season had opened—it was time to catch the season's biggest trout or shut up and stay shut up. Our decision was unanimous—we stayed sacked in the seclusion of our tent. We were all self-conscious—afraid we'd be laughed out of camp if we failed to catch a grandpappy trout on every cast.

Probably we'd still be hiding but for Wipala Wiki, the ageless Hopi Indian in charge of the crafts lodge. He slipped into our tent, and greeted us with: "How: O mighty-might fishermen of the Sit-Down Patrol!"

I was half out of the sack before realizing who it was. "Listen, Junior," I yelled. (Since he pretends he can't remember our patrol name, I downgrade him from his real title of Chief.) "State your business and vanish!"

"Yeah, Junior," said Toby, who was trying to figure how we could get chow without leaving our tent. "Hurry up so us brains can get back to important business."

"Me borrow fishing tackle?" Wiki asked.

93

"Sure," I said, pulling some gear from beneath my cot. "Help yourself. But cut that poor Indian dialect. It always spells trouble." Everyone knows that Wiki can speak perfect English when he wishes.

"Didn't know you were a fisherman, Junior," piped up Tommy Thompson.

Wiki didn't answer, nor was there the sign of a smile on his face. But his black eyes were laughing so that no stoic Indian would have admitted him to the tribal council.

Taking his time, Wiki selected a spool of good test line, a snelled hook, a shot-weight, and bobber—stuff I use for pan fish.

"Okay, I go now," he said, continuing to speak in Indian dialect.

"Hey, wait!" Beans said loudly, getting up. "What are you going to do with that gear? If you want to catch trout, take my rod and reel."

Wiki shook his head. "Me catch bigger trout with this outfit. Easier to carry, too," he added, stuffing everything into his pocket.

"You're crazy!" Beans roared. "No self-respecting trout will bite on junk like that."

The Tailbone Patrol voiced its unanimous endorsement of Beans' statement, which it now seems is just what that cagey old Indian thought would happen.

"I catch bigger fish!" Wiki stubbornly insisted. "Sit-

Down boys catch bedsores. Talk big fish! No catch 'em!"

"Is that so!" yelled Toby, fighting to get out of his sleeping bag.

"Billy!" I yelled at our hikemaster. "Draw grub, check us out! The Tailbone Patrol is going to educate this crazy Indian on the art of catching trout."

And so, two hours later, the Tailbone Patrol and Wipala Wiki were following the fisherman's trail down Tonto Creek toward the big holes below Bear Flats. The day was warm and we were perspiring freely—but not entirely from the heat. We were constantly running into groups of Scout fishermen, who lost no time ribbing us —"Bring out the yardstick, fellows. The Tailboners toss these minnows back."

Toby dropped back by me. "Guess we really asked for this razzing," he said. "And they're sure dishing it out!"

I nodded.

"But Mike," he pleaded, "don't just agree. You know we've got to catch a record-sized trout or keep on hearing these remarks, which are most unflattering to the Tailbone Patrol. Now quit being so calm and tell us how to catch a record trout. After all, you're the PL!"

Toby was still baiting me when Two-Bits Karsten joined us.

"I've got the answer right here, Mike," he insisted,

95

waving one of those fishing magazines under my nose. "Fish scents! The fish love 'em. You can't fail. Only costs five dollars. Let me run back to camp and order one."

"Five dollars!" murmured Beans Roberts. "All that dough and Two-Bits wants to spend it? I can't believe my ears."

"Tell me, Two-Bits," I asked, "did the fish write that ad?"

"Of course the fish didn't write the ad," he said patiently.

"Then how do we know this scent is irresistible to fish?" I demanded.

"I don't!" screamed the excitable Two-Bits, "but we'd darn sure better find some gimmick for catching fish, and right quick."

"Even if it takes five dollars?" queried Tommy Thompson.

"Yeah!" retorted Two-Bits.

"What do you think, Mike?" Toby asked. He had been reading the advertisement, and now had the magazine shoved under my nose. "It sure sounds like it'd do the trick."

I brushed the magazine aside and sat down. "First," I said, "I have the word of each of you—me included— that there're no finer fishermen in the state. Second, we all have some expensive new equipment we've never tried. We'll be in camp a month, and at least we didn't say what day we'd catch that record trout. So for this first day's fishing, let's just try it without fish scents, without panic, and without any more bragging."

"That's just what I was telling you, Two-Bits," said Beans Roberts.

"Aw, shutup," growled Two-Bits. "Just catch a fish as big as the one you bragged about last night."

Wipala Wiki, who had been listening to all this, started laughing.

"What's the matter, Junior?" growled Toby.

"The Tailbone Patrol stages the same sort of Donnybrook as the wrestling show on TV. Everyone blames everyone else. Any minute now we'll have a free for all. What a show! Ready cameras! Action!"

"Listen, Junior, we'd still be sacked out if you hadn't butted in. Now be careful. Savvy?"

"This old Indian has plenty of savvy," replied our cagey friend. Then he lapsed into that poor Indian dialect again. "Oh, Sit-Down Patrol, mighty fishermen, poor redskin honored to fish with you."

"Junior," I said, getting to my feet and motioning the patrol to get going. "Don't overtax our friendship. We might have to dampen you in one of these pools, if you make with any more sarcasm."

By midafternoon we reached Hell's Gate, where the Tonto goes tumbling through a deep, rocky gorge toward the desert lowlands. Here there were deep holes, filled, we hoped, with huge rainbow trout. And here also were no other Boy Scouts, which was a relief.

It was another hour before we pitched camp beside a huge pool below a troughlike waterfall. The pool was crystal clear, so deep it had a morning-glory hue and no visible bottom.

Packs came off; every Tailboner grabbed his trout pole, and rushed for a spot to cast from. Trouble was, there were too many bushes overlapping the pool's edge. In nothing flat we had our lines tangled up worse than an absent-minded square-dance caller. Immediately there was plenty of grousing, which only stopped when our Indian companion could control his laughter no longer. He roared, and furthermore he rolled on the ground, clutching his sides like he was in pain.

"Maybe Junior needs a tranquilizer pill," suggested Toby irritably.

"Haven't seen him even trying to catch a fish," pointed out Beans Roberts.

"How come, Junior?" I demanded. "This a put-up job to get us out of camp? Or do you intend to defend your challenge and catch a trout?"

Wiki controlled his laughter long enough to choke out an answer. "Me fish tomorrow. Sit-Down boys so noisy, frighten trout."

I hate to admit it, but he had us there.

"Okay, fellows," I said. "Tomorrow we fish for the big ones. Right now scatter out and fish for your dinner. That is if you guys want to eat tonight."

Everyone wanted to eat all right, but we did have to work for our supper. By dusk we had enough trout for a meal, but none were over fourteen inches. But who cared! We were catching fish, our new equipment was proving itself, we would soon be eating delicious, pan-fried trout as only Toby can cook them. Our spirits perked up. We felt good.

Back at our campsite we found that Wiki had chopped wood, had our cooking gear unpacked, our campsite cleaned.

"Well," spoke up Toby. "Looks like Junior's going to prove of some value on this trip."

"Keep up the good work and we might let you join the Tailbone Patrol," Billy Spears suggested.

Wiki turned and looked at him. "The Tailbone Patrol is not bashful when it comes to boasting that they are good campers. But what happens? They rush out to have fun fishing and leave all the camp chores to their guests. The guest is not pleased, so please excuse me if I am not overly eager to join your patrol."

"Independent, isn't he?" commented Tommy Thompson.

"But he's right," spoke up Billy. "As hikemaster, I should have stayed here and gotten the cooking gear in shape. And Mike should have appointed an assistant to get in the firewood."

"Junior," I said, "as a guest of the Tailboners, you have not been treated right. We apologize. Fellows, the first trout goes to Junior."

"What's the matter," Wiki demanded. "Fatso's cooking so bad you want me to test it first?"

"Mike!" Toby wailed. "I'm an artist with the fry pan, but I'm temperamental. Keep that Indian quiet or he'll be wearing this skillet as a metal headdress when I'm through with him."

"Why, Toby," I chided. "Watch your manners. He's our guest."

However, after Toby lifted the first golden brown trout out of the skillet and dropped it into Wiki's plate, relationships became friendlier. But not for long. Once Wiki was filled, he complimented Toby. But it was more like shoving the needle in deeper.

"Those trout were cooked perfectly, Fatso," Wiki said.

"Mike," pleaded Toby, "can't he call me stupid or clumsy, or anything but Fatso?"

"The description is tailormade for you," Beans Roberts pointed out.

"Is that so!" yelled Toby, who made a dive for Beans. The two started wrestling and rolling around—and—yep, they fell into the deep pool. In nothing flat they tumbled right out, teeth chattering as they made a dash for the fire, where Wiki was adding more wood.

"If you guys wanted a bath, you could have gone downstream," I suggested. "You'll frighten the fish, behaving like that."

"He's worried about the fish, when two of his patrol are freezing to death," grumbled Beans Roberts.

Now, despite all this horseplay, for once the Tailbone Patrol was dead serious about something—we had to catch a whale of a trout or get laughed out of Camp Geronimo. And the big test would come the next day. So, the Tailbone Patrol hit the sack early—and considering the results, it'll probably be the last time that minor miracle ever happens.

We were camped right beside Tonto Creek, which was recklessly plunging over the rim rock toward the desert. Huge canyon walls pinned us in, and the roar of the creek was like a Niagara Falls. You could close your eyes, but couldn't stop up your ears. Try as I could, it was impossible to get to sleep. I seemed to grow wider and wider awake. Finally, I got up. In seconds the rest of the Tailbone Patrol gathered around.

"Noisy hotel room tonight, boss man," said Billy.

"Quiet! You are disturbing my sleep!"

I recognized Wiki's voice. "Get him, fellows," I ordered.

In short order our protesting Indian was sitting by

102

the fire, and all Tailboners took up the task of keeping Wiki awake. I have no idea what time we finally gave up, but it was quite late. At any rate, we were all so tired we gradually dropped off to sleep in spite of Tonto Creek.

But our Indian guest had the last laugh. Somehow, he was up and about at five next morning. Naturally, no Tailboner ever thinks of opening an eye at such an hour. So, after getting the fire going, Wiki visited each of us, water canteen in hand. Just a little splash of water in the face and another Tailboner was sitting up grumbling. Of course, with Toby it took a full canteen.

Let's just pass breakfast by and say it was not a very cheerful meal.

Pancakes and cocoa down, the Tailboners grabbed their fishing gear and set off by twos to catch all the big trout in the canyon pools. Billy and Toby remained behind to clean up the breakfast dishes, and Wiki started chopping wood for our dinner meal.

"We'll do that," Billy insisted as he watched our guest wield an ax. "Maybe you'd better get started if you're going to live up to your promise and catch a bigger trout than the Tailbone Patrol."

"Yeah," muttered Toby, "or was that a come-on to get us dumbclucks out here in the open so everyone in camp could laugh at us when we return empty handed?"

Wiki looked at the two perturbed Tailboners and

grinned. "Sit-Down boys always blow a fuse in heavy storm," he said. "Old Indian saying, young bucks chase all directions looking for food. Go hungry. Old bucks sit patiently, game come to them. They have full stomach."

"Okay, old buck," Toby snorted. "You stay here with your pin and bobber. Billy and I are going to join the Tailboner anglers in quest of the monster of Tonto Creek."

"Yeah, man!" muttered Billy. "See you later, pan fisherman."

Now, I was fishing with Tommy Thompson, and Billy and Toby overtook us as we were eating our nosebag lunch.

"Where's Wiki?" I asked.

"Back at camp," said Toby. "Said he'd fish there. You fellows had any luck yet?"

"Plenty of small stuff," I replied. "You?"

"Same," snorted Billy.

"Fellows," Toby said, "this situation is getting so desperate that I'm beginning to wonder if Junior has something up his sleeve that perhaps we should know about."

"And if he has, how'll you get him to spill the beans unless he wants to?" I demanded.

Billy patted his field glasses. "As chief supply man, I'm equipped to the hilt, boss man."

"I don't like to spy on him," I said doubtfully.

"We'll just fish back toward camp, and take an advance peek in on our Indian competitor," Toby reassured me.

And that is how things were.

It was about three-thirty in the afternoon when we reached a point where we could see our campsite. Billy took out his glasses and looked over the familiar terrain.

"See him?" Toby demanded.

"Naw! Wait! Why that lazy old snake-bait. He's sleeping by the pool."

"He's what?" growled Toby, grabbing for the glasses. "Why the. . . ." and then he started chuckling.

"What happened? You get tuned in on a different station?" I asked.

He handed me the glasses. "Some squirrels got in a fight in the pinyon tree over his head and a few nuts plunked Wiki on the noggin. He's shooing the squirrels away."

I focussed the glasses. Apparently the squirrels had been routed, for now Wiki was bending down and untying something from one foot, which was without moccasin. Then I saw him pull in a line, bobber, and hook. He looked at the hook, laid it aside, and went down stream to some rocks by the water's edge. After turning some rocks over he picked up something, returned, baited the hook, tossed hook and bobber into the pool, tied the string around his big toe, and lay back on the bank for a catnap.

All this I described to my fellow Tailboners.

Billy was the only one who made any sense. "I bet that was a hellgrammite he's baiting his hook with. Dad's told me they work sometimes when nothing else will."

"Well, he can't know much about trout," I retorted. "A little old eight-inch trout could sure snag that line around his big toe."

"Well, what'll we do?" Toby demanded.

"Why don't we sneak in real quiet, and see if we can't bait his hook with one of our fingerlings," Billy suggested. "Bet it'll be the first fish that old desert nomad ever caught."

We agreed, and that is how it happened that Toby, Billy, Tommy Thompson, and I were standing right behind Wiki when it happened. Honestly, if I hadn't been there I wouldn't believe it.

There was Wiki, one foot bare with a line attached to his big toe and a bobber riding nice and pretty out there in the big pool. And that old Indian was sure making up for lost sleep the night before. He was snoring like a steam locomotive running down grade.

"He'll probably keep us awake tonight and tell us we're not in condition like he is," I chuckled.

Toby was slipping out of his clothes. "Wait till I bait his hook with this minnow," he said. "Tommy, get your camera ready. We don't want to miss the tale of the mighty fisherman who. . . ."

Toby's voice was drowned by as wild an Indian warhoop as those staid old Arizona canyons had heard in eighty years. Wiki was sleeping no more!

"Wiki!" yelled Billy.

He had been lying flat on his back, his feet about two feet from the water's edge. When that line went taut, Wiki yelled, and braced himself into an upright position with his arms. As he reached over to grab at the line

107

fastened to his toe, he began bouncing toward the water like a basketball being dribbled.

"The bobber!" I shouted. "It went straight down!"

Then there came another blood-curdling Indian yell, then sudden silence. Wiki had hit the pool with a resounding splash, and had disappeared from sight.

In all parts of undress, four Tailboners hit the pool right after him.

"Spread out," I ordered. "He ought to surface soon, I hope."

Well, Wiki did surface, and there was plenty of red blood to mark the spot.

"My toe!" he yelled, gulping in a lung full of air as he ducked down toward his feet.

"He must have a whale on there," shouted Toby. "Don't let him cut that line!"

The Tailbone Patrol swam in on the quarry. No water polo match was ever rougher. Wiki was thrashing around like a wild man. In fact I came out of it with a shiner. But I got him in a cross-the-chest carry. Toby took him from the other side. And boy, did we have a struggle. Whatever it was pulling in the opposite direction was no slouch.

However, Billy had seen the problem and had gotten a stout piece of firewood, which he wrapped around the line. He and Tommy Thompson kept pressure on the firewood, easing up the drag on Wiki's toe.

When we got ashore, Billy Spears fastened Wiki's line to his reel, and tried reeling in the monster. I saw our quarry break far out in the pool, a huge rainbow which surfaced and shook himself like the champion he was, then sounded for the depths. "You land him, Billy," I commanded, "or Wiki and I'll feed you to the fishes for sure."

Then I turned my attention to that mangled big toe, and it was really in bad shape. I got the line cut away, Toby cut down some tongue depressors for splints, and using compresses and some antiseptic, we got the bandage on and checked some of the blood flow.

We were just in time to see Billy reel a very tired but still game trout over to the shallows. The fish looked like a freight car. Slowly Tommy Thompson slipped in behind him with a dip net. With a sudden scoop, and Billy reeling in, they slipped Mr. Grandaddy Trout out on the bank. We set up a yell. Even Wiki yelled.

"Get out the yardstick," I ordered. Billy already had his steel tape. "Twenty-nine inches," he yelled. "And that should shut up those doubting Thomases."

"Yeah!" I said, "but Billy, you just landed him. Wiki really caught him, on a line, shot-weight, bobber, and his big toe."

Wiki looked up startled. "Oh, no!" he pleaded. "If the Tailbone Patrol doesn't tell how I damaged my toe, I won't tell anyone that Billy didn't land that trout all the way. After all, we are on a Tailbone Patrol hike. One for all, and all for one, you know."

Well, that is how the next afternoon the Tailbone Patrol, fishermen deluxe, returned to Camp Geronimo with proof of our fishing skills. Of course there was some curiosity about my black eye, about Wiki's bandaged toe, and about how we did catch that twenty-nine-inch trout. But, as honorary Tailboner Wipala Wiki says, "It all happened in the family."

The Steam-Heated Hike

The Tailbone Patrol could be the hikingest patrol in the country if we didn't eat like horses and have to act like horses to pack all the chow, sleeping bags, and camp equipment we need. As Toby says, whenever a hike is mentioned, "In this advanced mechanized age, travel on foot appears a bit old-fashioned."

"You're the one Tailboner a rugged hike would be good for," I remarked caustically. We had been at Camp Geronimo, high up in the Tonto Rim country of central Arizona, for several weeks, and—except for our trout fishing expedition—our longest trek had been to the mess hall.

Billy Spears seized the opportunity to remind us that he was hikemaster. "This patrol came into being when Doc told us to get off our tailbones and do something. He'll be up here next week, and he's apt to dynamite us into action."

"But it gets so cold up here at night you'd have to pack

a steam-heated sleeping bag," grumbled Tommy Thompson.

"Sit-Down boys kinda nuts. Indian sleep out in winter, much snow, only one blanket."

The speaker, of course, was Wipala Wiki, whose big toe had completely healed.

"Well, Junior," Beans Roberts said, "perhaps you Indians have a lightweight answer to the mountains of food Toby eats."

Wiki, his ageless face breaking into a grin, nodded. "Indian savvy food problem okay."

"Hey, maybe this will be the answer to our financial problems," chimed in Two-Bits Karsten.

Toby, who had been stretched out on one of the workbenches taking a rest, sat upright. "See here," he shouted. "This conversation is getting seditious or subversive or something."

Foxy Walker, Patrol Leader of our rivals, the Cougar Patrol, had been listening. Now he put his big foot into the conversation. "I'll bet you Tailboners are chicken to take a hike with Wiki and travel with the same minimum supplies the Indians would carry."

"Who says we're chicken!" roared Toby.

And that is how it happened that the Tailbone Patrol and Wipala Wiki left Camp Geronimo on a three-day hike to the top of the Tonto Rim, where a nine-thousand-foot elevation made the nights icebox cold.

THE STEAM-HEATED HIKE

We had won one concession—a pack burro.

The matter of supplies had been left to Hikemaster Billy Spears and Wiki, who we had thought was our friend. However, we now had serious doubts. One large pot, one skillet, one cooking fork, spoon, flapjack turner, flour, salt, and pepper completed our grub list. Our camping gear consisted of a poncho and blanket apiece and several changes of socks. We were even limited to one ax.

"But, Junior," I wailed, "only one ax!"

"Boy Scouts save trees," our Indian friend replied. "One ax save many trees. And now," he said, "we have what you call shakedown."

"A what?" I demanded incredulously.

"Empty all pockets," Wiki commanded.

This time Toby was not the only Tailboner whose pockets were stuffed with candy bars. Wiki turned them all over to the Chief, our Scout executive and camp director.

"You keep," he said. "We travel like Indians. No need."

"Chief!" Toby pleaded, falling in a heap in front of our grinning camp director. "Is the doctor in camp? I feel faint!"

"Think how you'll feel three days from now," he answered unsympathetically.

"I *am*," muttered Toby as he stood up.

Foxy Walker ran in and snapped a picture of Toby. "What's that for?" the fat one demanded.

"That's the before photo of you for the before-and-after photo spread I'm making."

Toby made a grab for the camera and missed.

"That poor little burro," Toby said, pointing to our very lightly packed pack animal. "How is he going to carry the starving Tailbone Patrol back to food and civilization?"

Before anyone could reply, Billy shouted, "Tailboners, let's go!" and started up the steep rim trail.

Wiki, looking like the real Indian he was, in his blue jeans held up by a big silver and turquoise studded concha belt, a purple velveteen shirt with silver buttons, and his long black hair held back by a red sweatband around his head, picked up the pack burro's halter rope.

Most of the guys in camp were out to see us off, and they cut loose with more Indian yells than Custer's men heard as Sitting Bull's braves charged to victory.

Toby dropped in step with me. "Mike!" he wailed. "You're PL. Say something! Do something!"

"Why don't you save your breath?" I suggested. "We've got a stiff climb coming up."

The first four miles we followed Tonto and Horton Creeks, climbing out of the tall pines into thickets of towering Douglas fir and thick, bushy spruce trees. We collapsed by the headwaters spring of Horton Creek, having climbed two thousand feet. In the next mile we'd climb another two thousand feet, for the trail went right up and over the nearly perpendicular cliffs of Tonto Rim.

Wiki, who had been bringing up the rear, dropped the pack burro's halter rope and looked us over.

"Braves of Sit-Down Patrol kinda soft," he stated.

"If you mean we're pooped, you said a mouthful," muttered Two-Bits, who was busy trying to drink the spring dry.

"Indian drinks lots before, after trip, not during trip," he said. "You stop!"

Two-Bits sat back in surprise. Toby groaned and emptied the contents of his canteen on the top of his head.

"You braves rest. I go to grocery store," Wiki said.

"Sure, the nearest supermarket is a hundred miles away," Toby muttered, but Wiki paid no heed. He took the ax off the pack burro and struck off into the thick young growth of trees below the spring.

Tommy Thompson looked at me. "What do you suppose he meant?" Tommy demanded.

"How do I know?" I replied. "I'm just a tourist on this trip."

"But, Mike," Toby wailed, "I don't want to be an Indian chief."

"The Indians haven't slipped that far," retorted Billy.

115

"But say, fellows," he asked, "did you notice that Wiki wasn't even breathing hard, hardly sweating, and the Chief tells me he's over sixty years old?"

"Sixty?" I said in surprise, mopping the sweat from my forehead, as I fashioned a sweatband like Wiki's from my Scout neckerchief. "You kidding?"

"Nope," Billy replied. "Boy, we're going to have an experience."

"Chances are we'll never live long enough to apply for social security, much less live to collect our old-age pensions," Toby said. "This is a steam-heated hike that'll vaporize us."

"Hey, our grocery shopper's back," Beans said, pointing.

Wiki emerged quietly from the thicket, carrying a number of green branches about an inch in diameter and two feet long. Then I noticed that each stick was slightly bowed, in the general shape of an archer's bow.

"Maybe we're going to sample some delicious and appetizing oak stew," suggested Toby.

Wiki returned the ax to the burro's pack and then handed each of us one of the sticks.

"While rest, you whittle," he said. "Cut off top and bottom, so half-inch thick through middle."

"What is it?" Billy demanded. "Sounds like it'll be a boomerang."

"Sure, these Hopi Indians imported them years ago from Australia," Toby replied.

"Indian rabbit stick," Wiki said. "You throw straight, hit rabbit, we eat. No throw straight, tighten up belt."

"Aw, Mike," Toby wailed. "Even the buzzards won't be able to pick any nourishment off our bones."

I had my knife out peeling off the bark. "Start cutting," I said.

Wiki looked us over. "We go now, before muscle in leg get stiff, too much rest."

He didn't wait for us to stop our bellyaching. He picked up the halter rope and started up the trail. Still griping, we followed, but silently, for the trail over the Tonto Rim is so steep there's no use wasting breath talking.

Wiki and the burro were soon way in front. We had to use our hands as well as our feet to climb over the steep steps and sharp, pitched rocks of the trail. We were soon resting more than climbing, and Wiki and the burro were completely out of sight.

At one point I came upon Billy who was stretched out flat. He pointed to the vast Tonto Basin with its pine forests and grassy grazing lands stretched out in front of us for a hundred miles. "Just stopped for the view," he panted.

Then I noticed he had fashioned an Indian sweatband also.

"Good idea," he grunted, tapping his band.

Toby stumbled up to us. "Sixty years old, huh," he grumbled. "That Indian hasn't even been born yet."

117

Billy and I reached the top together. The few trees on the rocky rim were twisted and gnarled by the winds and deep snows. The wind blew strong up here and felt good.

We looked around but didn't see anyone.

"Over here," a voice called, and then we saw Wiki leaning against a rock by a grassy spot where the burro was grazing.

We staggered over only to find he had already finished whittling his rabbit stick.

We shook our heads and flopped down in the shade.

Wiki tossed some shavings on us. "Get busy, or no eat," he said.

"No wonder the Indians are a vanishing race," I said.

As was to be expected, Toby was the last Tailboner to reach the top. You could have squeezed water out of the sweatband around his head and from the shirt tied around his waist.

He flopped on the ground.

"If hikes like this become popular, the Indians will take over the country again. There won't be anyone else left," he grunted.

Wiki went over to the pack burro and came back carrying moccasins for each of us. We had been making them in the craft lodge, but hadn't finished them.

"I finish 'em last night while braves sleep," he said. "You put on, no more rocks, we hike quiet, no talk, see much."

The Tailboners all got up on their feet and walked around to test out their new moccasins. We stepped on dead twigs and dry leaves, and there was hardly a sound.

Wiki grinned. "Step out on toe, don't fall back on heel. Okay, we go now."

Billy took the halter rope and, with the burro, brought up the rear now. Wiki led the way and we followed single file, Indian fashion.

We hiked only a short distance before we were in a thick forest of fir and spruce, the north side of the trees covered with thick moss, and the ground a soft carpet of needles and grass.

We had just come to the old military road, along which the U.S. Cavalry had once shipped supplies from Fort Apache to Camp Verde, when Toby saw some old graves—four rock-marked graves and some inscriptions carved in the white bark of nearby aspen trees. We were able to make out "Indians. . . . 1884."

"Another seventy years and folks will find our graves with the same markers," Toby said grinning.

We crossed the road and started down a deer path that led to the grassy meadows alongside Turkey-Beaver Creek. Suddenly Wiki held up his hand. We froze in our tracks, and then we too saw the deer, a big eleven-point buck grazing on some buffalo grass. We weren't a hundred feet from him, and Toby grabbed for his camera.

Wiki motioned for Toby to join him at the front of the line.

He indicated that the rest of us were to stay still while he and Toby stalked the deer. Moving slowly from tree to tree, sometimes hardly moving a foot, they made their way toward the deer. Finally, they reached the edge of an aspen thicket, not twenty feet from the deer, and Wiki coughed softly. The buck lifted his antlered head, alert for danger. Toby snapped his picture, and as he did, the deer broke and disappeared in the woods.

We rushed forward.

"Wow!" Toby said. "What a picture. Boy, that's worth starving for. Wait until Pop sees that photo. He went hunting last fall and never got close enough to a buck to take a shot."

Our guide laughed. "Indian see much on hike. Learn much. Have much fun."

"You said it," Beans Roberts replied. "I never saw a deer that close in a zoo."

In a few minutes we were out of the trees into the knee-high grass of the high mountain meadows. For over an hour we hiked along the deer path that ran near the creek. One of the things that makes the Tonto Rim so unusual is that the land at the top all slopes away from the rim. So, the stream we were following was at first small, but, as it was fed by numerous springs from the side hills, it soon became fair-sized.

Suddenly the grass in front of us waved and an animal started running toward a distant clump of aspen trees.

"Porcupine," Wiki yelled. "Rabbit sticks!"

The Tailbone Patrol went charging through that grass like a bunch of Indians, whooping and yelling. We circled the porcupine, keeping a most respectful distance. Then, at a signal from Wiki, we all threw our rabbit sticks at the spiny animal.

At least two sticks scored direct hits and stretched the animal out. Wiki rushed in and clubbed the porcupine, then promptly set about skinning him with his hunting knife.

"Look at that guy's pincushion," Toby said, gingerly poking the porcupine's tail and exposing the fishhook-like needles. Carefully he extracted a few porcupine quills and stuck them into his hat.

"Nature boy, that's me," he said.

"Is a porcupine good to eat?" Beans asked.

Wiki nodded. "Like a fat piece of pig. We roll him in mud, bury him in hot coals in ground, have roast pork tomorrow."

"Let him cook all night?" Two-Bits asked.

Wiki nodded.

"But I can't wait that long for chow," Toby wailed. "I'm starving."

Wiki pointed to a high piece of ground down the valley. "Make camp beneath those trees. Get firewood. Clean out spring by clump of trees. Get going."

There was a spring by the clump of trees, just as Wiki said there was, and by the time he had finished cleaning the porkie, we had camp pitched. He salted down the porcupine and hung it from a tree branch.

"Now we go look for dinner," he said, picking up his rabbit stick. We grabbed ours and followed.

"Half go over to edge of woods, other half start by creek. Go slow, beat grass, yell, keep moving toward each other. Maybe we get rabbit."

In a half-hour we had four fat rabbits. Our Indian tutor assigned the task of cleaning them to Toby. Then he sent Beans and Two-Bits out with the big pot to pick dandelion greens. He sent Tommy back on the trail we had used to pick wild strawberries in a patch we had passed. Then he gave me a drop line and hook and a trout fly. "You go down to creek; catch trout for breakfast."

You know, I've never had such fishing. Guess anglers just don't like to hike fifteen miles to catch fish. None of mine were big fellows, mostly nine and ten inches long, but I soon had enough for breakfast. I cleaned them, wrapped them up in grapevine leaves, and then weighted them down with rocks just below our spring.

When I came into camp, a slit trench had been dug with sharpened sticks, lined with fire rock, and a bed of hot coals lay in the trench. Wiki brought in our porcupine, covered in an inch of mud, dropped it in the coals, and raked coals all around it. Then he covered it all over with dirt, packing it down tight.

"Be ready noon tomorrow," he said.

By a tiny fire he had Beans cooking the rabbits in the skillet and keeping an eye on the boiling pot of dandelion greens.

"See where porcupine strip bark from aspen trees," Wiki said. "Get big slabs of bark. No have to wash dishes tonight."

"Boy, I'm liking this hike better every minute," Toby said.

Fried rabbit, dandelion greens, and strawberries for dessert—not bad for an empty packsack gang. Even Toby had enough to eat.

By now the sun was down, the first pale evening stars were out, and the tops of the tall firs and spruce were like black spires against the night sky. From the distance a coyote howled, and we nervously tossed more wood on our campfire.

Wiki shook his head. "Scouts burn much wood; Indian use little fire."

"But, Junior," Tommy Thompson said, "it's cold up here. Need a fire to keep warm; at least us paleface braves need a fire."

"Yeah," I said. "How are we going to keep warm with only one blanket apiece? I'm shivering now."

"You wait," Wiki said. "Me show."

Well, believe me, that was some campfire. The Tail-boners huddled around the fire, and listened to legends of the Hopi Indians and their lives in mesa-top villages.

We could have sat listening to Wiki all night, except for one thing. We were cold. If we were warming our front side, our back side had icicles on it. Besides, that little campfire wasn't big enough for all of us to get around at one time.

Between chattering teeth, Toby said, "Boy, I hope Junior can solve this sleeping problem as capably as he solved the grub situation."

"Well, I'm betting on him," I replied.

"Me, too," replied Two-Bits Karsten, "since there's nobody else on this hike who could solve this problem for us."

"Hey, he's showing us how to fix our beds," Beans called.

Using a pointed stick, Wiki scooped out a space in the soft, moist ground the size of his body and about six inches deep. Soon we were all digging and then building a fire in the impression we had dug, just as he was doing.

And those fires sure felt good.

"Boy, I'm warm for the first time tonight," Toby said. "Guess the landlord heard we were freezing and sent up some heat. But what goes now?"

Wiki had let his fire burn down to a bed of coals and was now scraping the dirt over the coals, and tromping down the dirt.

"Oh, boy," Tommy Thompson yelled, "nature's electric blanket."

Like a bunch of dogs digging for rabbits, we scraped the dirt over the coals and packed it down. With the coals covered up, it was cold in the night air and we made a dive for our blankets, wrapped ourselves up in them and lay down.

"Ow!" yelled Beans Roberts, as he leaped upright. "I'm scorched."

It didn't take the rest of the Tailboners long to understand Bean's problem. It was like trying to sleep on top of an old wood stove that was red-hot.

We looked at Wiki, squatting down by the tiny campfire, whittling on another rabbit stick.

We walked over and joined him. "Guess the heat will let up soon," I said, hoping I'd get a reply, but he paid no attention.

For the next half-hour, about every two minutes one of us would dash over and feel his bed to see if it was still too hot to sleep on.

It was quite dark, and we were quite cold when we realized that after one such trip, Toby hadn't returned. A quick inspection showed him curled up in his blanket, the ground cloth over him to keep off the morning dew.

"Like a bug in a rug," he said. "Climb in."

And we did.

"Boy, this is great," sang out Tommy Thompson. "Anybody want to buy my sleeping bag when we get back to camp?"

It was nice and warm in the blanket, but soon I realized that something was wrong. I felt wet and clammy. I lifted an edge of the blanket, and the cool air felt like a breath off a snowbank. Then I realized what the trouble was. We hadn't waited long enough for the hot coals to cook all the moisture out of the damp earth, and that moisture was coming up into our beds like live hot steam.

I was already wet with sweat and wondering what to do when Toby suddenly erupted like a live volcano.

He shot up in the air and shook himself free of blanket and covering groundcloth like a dog shaking water after a swim.

"I'm being scalded, slowly but surely," he yelled. "I'm in a Turkish bath. I'm sweating off pounds, including a good portion of raw flesh and skin."

Everybody laughed, including the burro.

But suddenly, free from the live steam and wet blanket, Toby started to shiver.

"I'll freeze to death," he roared.

"Come over here!"

It was Wiki, who, as soon as the commotion started, had tossed a lot of firewood on the campfire, which blazed up high.

In jig time the entire Tailbone Patrol was standing around the fire getting warmed up.

Wiki went over and carefully tested the dirt over his bed. Apparently the steam had stopped rising from the ground, for he carefully wrapped himself up in his blanket and groundcloth.

"Goodnight, Sit-Down Patrol," he called out. "Too

bad you didn't follow directions. Perhaps in an hour your beds will be dry like mine."

"This some sort of Indian joke?" Toby asked, edging his backside closer to the fire.

"Young braves make many mistakes," Wiki replied. "But Indian way, they make same mistake but one time."

"And how," Beans Roberts retorted.

It was about an hour before our beds were dry enough to lie down on and before our blankets had dried out. By that time we were sure of one thing. The Indians had the answer to the problem of traveling light, but to learn how to do it was a risk you took at your own peril. But the Tailboners were used to living dangerously, and we loved it.

Toby's Ordeal

The pick-up truck rattled down the gravel driveway of the R Bar C Ranch before it stopped at the horse corrals. The noisy barking of hound dogs left no doubt that this late visitor was Floyd Haught, government lion hunter.

"Must be something unusual to bring Floyd out this time of night," said the Chief, our Scout Executive. "Let's give him a hand!"

Thirty Scouts dashed from the main ranchhouse, pulling on jackets as we ran, for even in summertime the nights are cold in Arizona's high Tonto Basin country. Each one of us, during our growing-up years at Camp Geronimo, had known Floyd Haught and his lion dogs. Floyd was a bit of the authentic old west, and we counted it a personal privilege to know him.

His coming was really heaping reward on an already bountiful evening. We were all members of the Wipala Wiki Lodge of the Order of the Arrow, and had that night tapped eight candidates for membership. And now, at nearly midnight, we had just returned from leaving these hopeful candidates bivouacked alone for their night's ordeal, their solo camp-out. "Taps" meant nothing for us tonight, so we had been enjoying coffee and hot chocolate and comparing notes on where we had left our respective candidates for the night.

Now, usually I wouldn't be caught dead with Foxy Walker, Patrol Leader of the Cougar Patrol, but tonight was different. When the chips are down, Foxy and I are both Troop 10'ers. And one of those Order of the Arrow candidates was Toby. Foxy and I were both splitting our buttons because Troop 10 was adding another member to Scouting's honor camping society.

Foxy and I had personally taken charge of Toby's ordeal. No one was going to say we were soft on one of our own. That's why we had hiked Toby half-way to the top of the Tonto Rim, and on a windswept ledge somewhere near the 8,000-foot elevation, surrounded by sheer cliffs, had left our candidate to his lonely personal vigil. (It's amazing how a guy gets to know himself better when he's alone under the stars.)

Foxy and I were the last Order of the Arrow members to return to the R Bar C Ranch. The ranch brand stands for Roosevelt Council, and on this cattle ranch Explorer Scouts brand calves, mend drift fences, put out salt blocks, operate a sawmill, and do all the other tasks

131

of cattle ranching. It's a swell place, and it looked particularly great to us that night. We crowded around the old pot-bellied stove and got some hot chocolate from a steaming GI can. We were drinking the chocolate and starting to warm up when Floyd arrived.

"Sure will be great to see old Floyd," panted Foxy as we dashed between the meathouse and the tack room down by the corrals. "Heard he was over on the East Verde chasing the latest range killers."

Down at the corral, Floyd was patiently greeting each Scout by name, shaking eagerly offered hands; and all the while the pack of hound dogs cooped in the wire cage in back of the lion hunter's pick-up truck were howling their heads off.

"Hey, Mike! Mike Peterson and Foxy Walker!" Floyd called. "Can you guys water my hounds and feed 'em? Maybe the Chief here will let you put 'em in an empty hoss stall for the night."

Naturally Foxy and I were pleased at being selected, and rushed over to the truck. We knew Floyd would have each dog on a leash, and that on the front seat of his truck we would find a snap chain to which we could fasten each dog's leash. Also, somewhere amid Floyd's gear would be the rations of dried meat he fed his lean, eager hounds.

The hounds set up an awful clamor when we took them from the truck. Old Lead Dog jumped out first, followed by Red, Blackie, and two pups, Buster and Louie.

At our inquiry about two missing hounds, Floyd laughed. "Naw, nothing serious happened to Spic or Span. Them brainless dogs just got too close to a skunk family to make good traveling companions, so they're back at the home ranch airin' out."

Foxy and I had fed the dogs and watered them, and were spreading some loose hay over the floor of an empty stall for the dogs to bed in, when Floyd and the Chief entered the barn. Foxy nudged me when he saw them coming. Something in their manner, the set of their faces, their rapid strides, spelled trouble, serious trouble.

"Where did you Scouts leave Toby?" the Chief asked abruptly.

"On the side of Promontory Butte," I replied. "Perhaps a mile beyond where the Highline Trail crosses the trail out of Horton Creek thicket. Why?"

The Chief ignored my question. He glanced at Floyd. The old lion hunter, his leathery face furrowed and unsmiling, nodded solemnly. "That's plumb in line with the killer's path," he said. "Guess we'd better saddle up and start riding tonight."

"What's this all about?" Foxy asked.

"Don't want to alarm you boys," Floyd said. "But your pal may be in trouble. I been chasing an old tomcat over by the East Verde. He's an old cat, lame in a front

133

foot. Got a paw caught in a trap once. This winter he couldn't cover his hunting range like when he was younger. Instead of covering a sixty- to seventy-mile run, he had to settle for a smaller and smaller area. When he got real hungry, he started killing cattle as well as deer. Then late this spring, over at Logan Ranch, this old tom got into a corral and killed a colt. One of the

cowboys shot him, but the old cat got away. However, that shot slowed him down even more. He couldn't catch game, as he had before. He got thin, and hunger made him dangerous in an unusual way for a mountain lion. A hungry cat gets desperate. This week he killed a fisherman's dog over on the East Branch. The whole affair plumb frightened this trout fisherman near to pieces.

"That's when the Forest Service called for me and my dogs. But this is a wise old cat. I been chasing him three days now, and the best me and the dogs have done is drive him out of his usual territory. Now tonight, just before dark, I got a shot at him. We were following his tracks in back of the Zane Grey cabin, when I saw him sneaking over the top of the cliffs above the clearing. Just got one shot, but I hit him. A couple minutes later, though, I caught a glimpse of that old tom heading east along the Highline Trail. . . ."

"Right toward Toby's bivouac spot!" Foxy Walker exclaimed.

"That's right!" Floyd said. "It was too dark for me and the dogs to check on that cat, up there among those rocks. But I'm sure he's wounded. Now a hungry, wounded tomcat can be bad business."

"Let's go, Chief!" I said quickly. "Foxy and I will saddle the horses."

The Chief nodded. "Come on, Floyd," he said. "You could stand a cup of hot coffee before we leave. And I want to get my rifle."

When Foxy and I left him, high on the windswept face of the Tonto Rim's pink and white cliffs, Toby had been hunched down in the lea of a towering rock, out of the direct force of the wind. I knew that he wasn't frightened at being left alone. Instead, he was proud and happy at the honor he had truly earned. But later, after all that happened that night, he told me how it was.

He had watched our flashlights as we picked our way down the stony ledge toward the trail. The trail would lead down several thousand feet into the sentinel-like spikes of the pine and fir forest that lay like a spiny black carpet far beneath him. Farther to the south were a few pinpoints of light Toby judged to be Kohl's Ranch and the campgrounds for summer fishermen. Way to the south, silhouetted against the night sky, was the shadowy mass of the Pinal Mountains and the winking of an airline beacon.

After regaining his breath, for the climb had all been up grade, Toby looked around. He was on a rocky shelf, cut off on three sides by high cliffs. He found that the wind was less severe beside the upper cliff. There were only a few twisted pine and mountain oak trees growing on the narrow ledge; also a few century plants, but little other suitable materials for firewood. It took Toby an hour to pull dead branches off trees, to break off the dead stalks of the century plants, to pull a few tufts of dead bunch grass from between cracks in rocks.

Toby was exhausted when he finished gathering his small supply of firewood. He had to rest. His only large piece of wood was a dead pine tree that he had pulled from the narrow rocky crack where it had grown, by using his weight for extra leverage on the end of his Scout rope made fast to the tree top.

Rocks were plentiful, so Toby built a rock wall as a windbreak for his fire. He soon had a blaze started, and crowded close, letting the welcome warmth penetrate his chilled body. However, he allowed the fire to burn into a bed of coals, and then fed the fire slowly to conserve his fuel supply.

The fire had been placed well as had the windbreak. The windbreak reflected the heat against the cliff's sheer face. This enabled Toby to sit a few feet from his fire, to enjoy its warmth, and yet not have the fire's glow mar his vision of either the earth spread out beneath him, or of the universe extending limitlessly overhead.

It was a clear night, and the luminous band of the Milky Way seemed just beyond his outstretched hand. It was, he thought, as though he sat on a platform in space, gazing through the one hundred billion stars of our great galaxy, the Milky Way, to the thousands of other galaxies that lay beyond in that great abyss of intergalactic space.

With the heavens seeming so near, Toby found it extremely difficult to believe what he had learned in science class that year. What he was actually doing, he knew, was looking far into distance and back into time. Each tiny pinpoint of light, which he saw as a star, was actually sunlight reflected by stars that were a hundred or a thousand times the size of our sun, a very minor star in our great galaxy.

Toby stirred, stretching a leg that had fallen asleep. Then he turned to reach a piece of wood to place on the fire. At that moment, in the charred shadows beyond the circle of flickering firelight, a movement, more sensed than seen, moored his eyes to the spot.

The spot where the motion had occurred was at the open end of the ledge, between Toby and his only way to the outside world.

The movement had to be that of an animal, he reasoned. A fairly large animal. But what animal would be climbing over the cliffs of the Tonto Rim? More to the point, what animal would lurk beside a human camp, especially one with a campfire burning? What kind? A crazed animal! One driven by hunger! One dangerously wounded!

Not a pleasant prospect, Toby realized, and he shivered from more than the cold.

Then there was nothing to do but watch and wait. As each intolerable minute unreeled from the endless spool of his nightmare, his fears rose. Would this waiting never end? Was it true? Had he really seen something? Was he now questioning his own veracity? Perhaps this solo camp-out, this ordeal, this lonely vigil, was causing him to imagine things. He had heard or read of such things happening. Was it happening to him? Had it already happened? Just now!

Then, as unreasoning fear and uncertainty sapped his strength, he saw the smoldering eyes, felt their angry glower pin him down like sharp fangs. He was indeed trapped, with no avenue of escape, and suddenly Toby could hide himself from his fears no longer. With a groan of dismay he let his arms fall to his sides, a gesture of defeat. And there mounted within him a resentment at being left isolated in this hopeless situation, for he felt completely abandoned—alone.

With fear printed upon his whole person, even Toby's normal actions became disjointed, uncertain. He tried to move, but his feet were fastened in the mortar of his fear. He tried to cry out for help, but no sound passed his lips; besides, there was no one to hear, even if he could cry out. Even before an attack came, if one did come, Toby was defeated.

"Do you give up in a situation like this?" he asked himself angrily. But where do you turn for help? He recalled his father saying that it took a world war to teach him how to pray. The Scout Oath and Law spoke of God and reverence. Toby prayed.

Then one of the Scout Laws—a Scout is Brave—entered his mind. He repeated it to himself: A Scout is Brave! A Scout is Brave! Like a pep rally, growing louder and louder, the words grew bolder and bolder, building his courage.

"The guy who wrote that Law sure isn't out here tonight," Toby groused to himself. The irony of his thoughts brought forth a tension-releasing chuckle.

Right you are, his inner voice told him. Nobody's out here to be brave for you. So, it's your life at stake. Say, didn't it mean anything to you; all those times you've repeated the Scout Law, saying A Scout is Brave? You some kind of fraud or something?

Slowly, as though being pried out of quicksand, Toby regained his physical and mental control. Then, in sudden haste, he turned to the task of weighing the facts, known and unknown, of his precarious situation. Every possibility, each alternate course of action, had to be evaluated for its possibility of success or failure. And out of these judgments, which he alone had to make, might lie a course of action that offered some hope.

He laid out his weapons, a Scout hatchet and knife. Then he considered what was perhaps his most effective weapon—fire. He scraped the bed of coals into a concentrated pile, pulling rocks around the coals to keep the wind from fanning them too quickly into spent ashes. He carefully surveyed his remaining supply of firewood, estimating its burning time. There was hardly enough to last until sun-up. Also, it would be several hours after sun-up before he could count on anyone returning for him. He had to save as much firewood as possible for use in case he was attacked.

Also, in the back of his mind, since it was not momentarily an urgent problem, he filed away the thought that he should find a way to forewarn anyone coming for him of the lion's lurking presence.

For he was now certain that this was a mountain lion. Probably two hundred pounds of tawny strength, which would measure at least seven feet in over-all length. A cat, sure-footed, quick of movement, with terrible claws probably eight inches across in full spread, and sharp teeth.

This momentary mental picture of his adversary drained Toby's strength, and left him shaken and frightened again. He roused himself once more from the stupor of fear, struggling to clear his mind of these frightening details of his adversary's physical advantages. He was a boy, a Scout, and he had little more than his human brain and Scout training to pit against his adversary's brute strength and cunning. But he had man's instinct and will to protect himself. He kept assuring himself that he could come through okay.

The next thing Toby surveyed was the security of his position for defense. He was up against a cliff that towered too high for attack from above. The cliff in front, which dropped away for several hundred feet, was but fifty feet away. There was no room for the cat to charge or spring from that direction.

Toby had entered his campsite from the direction now blocked by the lion. He knew there was ample room in that direction for the cat to spring and attack. Another one hundred feet beyond his campsite the ledge ended—so there was but one way in and out.

Toby's decision was made easy. Stay where he was, by the bed of live coals.

With his mind focussed on these live coals, Toby suddenly had an idea. He stripped a piece of leather off the elbow of his jacket. Using his Scout knife, he punched two holes through the leather at opposite ends. Through these holes he strung strips of his neckerchief, which he cut with his knife. When he was finished he had a slingshot; not the common pull type, but the throw type, like the one Biblical scholars say David used to slay the giant Goliath.

Toby said another prayer. His courage was returning. He found new strength.

Reaching around his feet, he found a small stone of the size and shape to fit his weapon. He placed it in the pocket of the sling, whirled the sling around his head to get momentum, and then let go of one of the twin thongs. The stone, traveling with tremendous force, reached the target but was wide of the mark. A few minutes of practice and Toby was reasonably accurate with the sling. But he didn't falsify his situation with wishful thinking. He wasn't apt to hit his target with this sling, but he had reasonable expectations of coming close enough to frighten or slow down his enemy.

There suddenly came a lull in the wind. Where there had been an avalanche of sounds as the wind swept over the rim rocks, the night was now hushed and strangely quiet. Overhead the stars seemed to dim, as the sky tightened with the predawn darkness. And Toby's fire seemed but a feeble effort to hold back the inevitable.

It was in this moment that the lion, his tawny body twitching nervously, stood out from the shadows of the cliff, and was now plainly visible to Toby. At the sight of the huge animal, all of Toby's hope collapsed. He sank back against the cliff face, pressing against the rock in fear.

His movement did not escape the lion. The head whirled, those glowering eyes pinned him tighter to the rock. The big cat's lips writhed back, and a low snarl battered against his bared teeth.

Then, as though sensing that Toby was momentarily taken care of, the big cat turned his head again toward the direction of the trail.

Regaining his composure, Toby carefully selected a flat stone. With a twig he pulled a live coal from the fire bed, and dropped it into the pocket of the sling alongside the stone. Straightening up, he whirled the sling around his head. With all his might he made his throw at the lion. The stone hit a boulder in back of the lion and ricocheted, spent and harmless, beneath the lion's tail. This startled the cat. But it was the red hot coal, blazing like a fiery eye in the dark, that now held his attention.

The lion grunted and growled, and then spit catlike at the coal. He sniffed at the coal, and convinced himself that it was his dreaded enemy—fire. Carefully, he circled around the coal, his eyes now riveted on this new factor.

That was when Toby saw the blood on the flank of the lion. The big cat was wounded, seriously enough that his right hind leg appeared to drag.

As the cat struggled to understand this new turn of events, Toby pushed one of the larger branches of firewood into the coals. At the same time he placed another stone in his sling.

Carefully now, working by instinct and feel rather than sight—never once taking his eyes off the big mountain lion—Toby built up his supply of rocks for the sling.

But again the cat chose to ignore Toby, turning his attention to some sound or scent coming from the direction of the trail, as yet undetected by Toby. The cat's tail switched back and forth, in mute testimony to the tensions and fears that gripped him.

Toby rummaged his thoughts for hope. What was the meaning of this? Why didn't the old tomcat retrace his steps? He could get off this ledge and bypass Toby's campfire easily. It wasn't more than a half-mile along the ledge to the trail. Why was the cat waiting?

As he thought through this problem, Toby's mind seemed strangely calm. He knew mountain lions seldom attacked human beings. Certainly if this cat intended to do so, he would have sprung at him long before this. Why, then, was the cat behaving this way?

Suddenly the cat seemed more agitated. He glanced at Toby, and roared, a fierce crescendo of fear and threat. And then he started dragging himself over toward the edge of the ledge, as though to circle around Toby, keeping as great a distance between them as possible.

But there was no place for the cat to go in that direction, and Toby did not want the lion so close to him. Moving with great speed, Toby again slipped a live coal into the sling, alongside the flat stone already there. He whirled the sling around his head, and let fly. The hot coal and stone both fell right in front of the nervously advancing lion.

The cat pulled back, spat at the coal, and growled angrily. Then he suddenly whirled and faced back toward the trail.

Was there something out there in the darkness? Toby remembered that the summer before he had heard Floyd Haught say that a lion will wait until the very last minute to make up its mind that the dogs are really after it.

And not until convinced beyond a doubt that he is the dogs' quarry, will a cat break and run.

And then Toby heard what undoubtedly the old tom had heard for some minutes. Off in the distance chimed the deep, sonorous, and lonesome voice of a trail-wise lion dog hot on a scent. And there followed a chorus of sharp, short, excited yappings as the rest of the pack of hounds caught the fresh scent discovered by the lead dog.

In his state of fright, Toby wondered if his mind was playing a trick on him. But he knew instinctively, by the nervous actions of the lion itself, that a pack of trained lion hounds was nearby. Grabbing a blazing branch from the fire, Toby stood waiting, fearful that, caught between two enemies, the lion might bolt and run in his direction.

The old tomcat crouched lower and lower, the twitching, tawny body drawn up like a taut spring about to be released. But Toby noted that the wounded leg would not draw under the body, in normal manner. The cat glanced at that damaged leg several times, then gazed long and steadily at Toby and beyond him at the remainder of the ledge.

Although he now felt a little sorry for the lion, wounded and cornered, Toby fitted another stone to his sling. He was, with the increasingly clear chorus of the hounds, quite aware that a moment of decision would be upon the big cat any second now.

And then it came. A tawny red hound dog, a fast blur in the firelight, darted in and snapped at the lion's wounded leg. The big cat whirled quickly, hissing and snapping at the dog. Toby heaved the burning branch, which he had pulled from the fire, at the cat. It almost landed on top of the cat, which roared in fright and anger. The dog rushed in, expecting the lion to be occupied with the fire. The big cat's massive forepaw caught the head of the dog a powerful but glancing blow, sending the yowling dog crashing against the cliff's sheer face.

The rest of the pack of yapping dogs, ready for the kill, came thundering across the ledge, ringing the old lion, worrying him, forcing him in this limited area to defend himself from all sides at once. And now in the distance Toby could hear the shouts of Floyd Haught and the Chief, of Foxy and me.

Toby's every muscle quivered and tensed as he watched each dog worrying the lion, holding it at bay. First one and then another would dash in, retreating at the last second, remaining just out of reach of those flashing widespread claws.

Now Toby could see our flashlights approaching. And then he heard the rifle shot. He saw the big cat shudder, then slump over as the dogs pounded in on their quarry.

There was for Toby a moment of sheer joy at deliverance. And then the tenseness, the knots of fear that had bound him, had harassed him, released their grip. It was as though there was no longer a bone in his body. Toby slumped down against the cliff face and slid slowly to the ground. It was at this moment that we reached his campfire.

The Chief got to Toby first, and supported his head in the crook of his arm.

"I'm okay! I'm okay!" Toby insisted.

"You sure are!" the Chief agreed.

"Never knew hound dogs could sound so wonderful," said Toby, grinning at Floyd.

"Bet they sure did sound welcome." Floyd grinned back. "That old tom was bad wounded. Don't think the old warrior really knew himself, right up to the end, what he would do next. Guess he was like some folks, afraid to go back, too tired to go on."

Toby looked up at Foxy and me. "Good thing you guys were a bit early returning for me," he said. "I might just have blown this ordeal all to pieces."

The Chief tousled Toby's head. "We're glad we got here, too," he said. "And we're ready to tell all the Order of the Arrow lodge members that they have a real Scout to welcome into the membership."

The Curse
of the Indian Chief's
Honorable Ancestor

Lots of smart folks claim they don't believe in superstition, but that's because no supernatural spirit has ever floored them.

The Tailbone Patrol started learning about superstitions on the day we checked out of Camp Geronimo. We were nuts, of course, to be leaving the mile-high, mountain-cooled, pine-scented camp a month before school started. But back in the very hot Valley of the Sun we had paying jobs.

We had recently gotten acquainted with the archeologist for the City of Phoenix. He does some urban renewal work on Pueblo Grande, the 1,000-year-old Hohokam Indian dwelling located within the city limits. This friend recommended us as pick and shovel laborers for a University of Arizona Archeology Department expedition. It planned to scrape off the top soil and look at the floor plan in a big Hohokam apartment complex just discovered along the lower Gila River. We were to receive room and board and folding money, and it was this get-rich-quick dream that led to our undoing.

Our first inkling of trouble came as we were getting ready to leave Camp Geronimo. Wipala Wiki spotted us as we waited for the Phoenix bus.

"Ho! Ho!" he said, his voice laughing, but his stoic face expressionless. "Sit-Down boys go home. We have good camp now, yes?"

"No!" we shouted.

Wiki adjusted the purple sweatband on his forehead. "I hear Sit-Down boys going to make Wipala Wiki's ancestors very angry. . . ."

"How come?" I asked.

"Sit-Down boys going to dig up ancestor's grave. Honorable ancestor not like that. Ancestor have great magic—put bad curse on Sit-Down boys."

Beans Roberts laughed. "Cut it out. This is a Hohokam mound we're excavating, and they pulled up stakes over a thousand years ago. Where they went the anthropologists don't know."

"Hohokam move north to Hopi Pueblos," Wiki said stubbornly. "This make Hohokam my ancestor. The first night you expose ancestor's bones, a coyote will howl. Then you know you find grave of Wipala Wiki's great-great-great-grandfather. Big medicine man. He place bad curse on anyone who disturb his resting place. You wait! You see! How do you say it? Pow on the kisser!"

Just then the bus arrived. "So long, Wiki," we called as we piled on. We couldn't tell if he was waving or shaking his fist at us.

As the bus left, Tommy Thompson sputtered a bit. "Aw, that old Indian's talking through his feather head-dress—I hope."

"You're probably right," agreed Toby with mock seriousness, "but we shouldn't overlook the truly mystical powers those old medicine men possessed. Now this curse might cause us some serious trouble. Who knows?"

Believe you me, Toby will never again joke about Indian medicine men and their curses. The Tailbone Patrol knows about such superstitions now. Leave 'em alone!

Our excavation site was 139 miles southwest of Phoenix, a half-mile from the Gila River, twenty miles from the nearest drinking water, thirty miles from a dirty irrigation ditch, where twice a week we could bathe away the dust of our archeology diggings. We were thirty-five miles from the nearest ice machine, and the daytime temperatures were just a little less intense than those at point of blast-off for a rocket launching.

The Gila River? Oh, out here in Arizona, all the people up-river siphon out the water, so downstream where we were you could walk across the dusty, sandy bed of this dried up river. Maybe that's why the Hohokams left. Smart Indians.

Anyway, at night when the sun went down and the air seemed cooler, we'd sit around on the adobe walls of the apartment house we were uncovering and gripe about the time it was taking for us to earn our first million bucks.

"Boy, I'd give a week's pay for an ice cold coke," Toby would mutter.

This always infuriated Two-Bits Karsten. "Mike," he'd plead, "do something about Toby. By my calculations he's already given up over five years' future pay for that bottle of coke. He's spreading the wealth faster than the Rockefeller Foundation."

About this time our boss, who wrote a letter each evening, would join our gripe session. There were twenty-four persons on the expedition, and the boss was Dr. Weatherford Jones, who taught archeology at the University. He knew an awful lot and always had a scientific-sized word for each new discovery we made.

He'd been a happy bachelor, I think. I don't know why at the age of forty he'd weakened and gotten himself engaged. The wedding was to be September 1, as our expedition ended August 31. He wrote a letter to the future Mrs. Jones every night, although the supply truck only went to town every other day. Man, Doc

Jones had the marrying bug bad, which qualified him to gripe along with the best of us Tailboners, as we sat there on the ancient peoples' dwellings.

Doc Jones told us we were making good progress, but he couldn't understand why we hadn't uncovered any burial grounds. Seems he wanted to bring his University classes to the site, but what's an Indian mound without a boneyard?

"We're half-way through August," I pointed out, and the good doctor knowingly took the bait.

"Just two weeks to go. Two more weeks," he sighed. "Must discover the burial ground by then . . . but if we don't! Can't postpone my wedding, you know!"

We applauded, but silently prayed he wouldn't find any burial grounds. But the very next day troubles fell upon us such as ordinary man had not known since the days of Job.

First, I'd better tell you how we excavated this archeological site. Once you uncovered the top of the walls—here they were volcanic rock set in adobe mortar—you slowed down to the speed of a weekend gardener. You probed in several places to see if you "hit" anything. If the results were negative, you then dug out six-inch layers across the room, a layer at a time.

We'd dug this room down about four feet, all probes negative. The sun was a blistering 120 degrees with no shade. Toby was carefully taking inch-wide slices with his shovel, and tossing the dirt onto a wire screen where we'd separate the dust from any artifacts.

Then Toby's shovel struck some unyielding object, so he pulled the blade from the ground. Doc Jones jumped into the diggings, and on their hands and knees these two scratched away some more dirt.

The first inkling the rest of us had of our impending disaster was Toby's wail, "Oh, no!"

While he sat back, an apprehensive look frozen on his face, Doc Jones' voice sounded rapturous—almost like he was talking about the future Mrs. Jones.

"Yes, boys, we've done it!" he chortled. "This is a human bone, a forearm, I think. Looks like we've been lucky and found a burial ground."

The Tailboners looked at each other in dismay.

"Gee! Did we have to do that?" muttered Beans Roberts, and his question was foremost in the mind of every Tailboner.

"Well," grumbled Two-Bits Karsten, "what is going to be is going to be. So we'll find out about Wipala Wiki's curse, that's all."

Doc Jones, sensing that we were somewhat less elated than he with this discovery, stood up and looked from one Tailboner to another.

"What's with you guys and this curse?" he asked.

So we told him.

He laughed heartily. "I think your Indian friend was

pulling your leg. In the first place, we don't know where the Hohokams went when they left these southern Arizona valleys. If your Indian friend has proof they settled what we now call the Hopi pueblos, he has more knowledge than the archeologists of America."

Doc Jones surveyed our faces again. "You Scouts don't really believe this Indian's yarn, do you?"

We shook our heads. You know, sometimes when confronted by the scientific mind, you hesitate to expose your unscientific fears. But that doesn't mean those fears have vanished—they're just being sat upon.

We all felt pretty much like Toby. "Doc Jones may be right, but then how does he know Chief Wiki isn't a descendant of the Hohokam? Isn't man a descendant of Adam?"

Tommy Thompson chimed in. "I bet that Wipala Wiki's receiving a transistorized seance report from his very, very mad ancestor right now."

Know what? Secretly, I think we all agreed with Tommy, but we didn't want Doc Jones to see this unscientific behavior and reasoning. After all, Doc Jones might be right, but he hadn't offered any proof that there's no such thing as an Indian curse strong enough to be hanging around a thousand years later. Had he?

All the rest of that day we scratched away little spoonfuls of dirt, and by evening we had partially uncovered four human skeletons. Doc Jones became very, very scientific. He photographed them from this angle and that angle. He sounded so much like the college professor he was that it became difficult for us nonprofessional types to communicate with him.

The time to knock off came and went.

"Looks like Doc Jones will be working by candlelight tonight," I observed sourly.

"I don't think so, boss man," said our weather wise hikemaster. "Sandstorm coming!" Billy pointed to the west.

Sweeping up the dry, sandy bed of the Gila River, so heavy it completely blotted out Signal Butte and the Castle Dome Mountains, was a towering brown turbulence, already reaching thousands of feet into the sky. This cloud of dust was blotting out the direct rays of the hot desert sun, and a false twilight was engulfing the vast expanse of desert. No mistake about it, we were in for a real blow.

"Hey, Doc Jones," I called, jumping into the excavated room beside him. "We'd better strike the tents before the storm hits."

He looked up. "Darn! Darn! Darn!" he moaned, casting a longing look at his boneyard.

"Get a canvas over this room," he ordered. "Weight the canvas down."

He called to the rest of his student crew. "Strike the tents and sit on 'em. Get towels over your faces. Keep nose and eyes covered."

157

"As soon as I get our camp secure, I'll be back to help protect our excavation!" he shouted.

We ran to get a tarp, usually used for shading a digging from the direct rays of the sun. As we started back up the incline to our diggings, lugging the heavy canvas, the first gusts of wind hit us.

The dust seemed to spurt out from under our feet. The heavier particles of sand, windblown, hit with such force they stung through our shirts.

By now the towering, angry, boiling, advancing wall of dust had blotted out the blue sky. The world had shrunken to a half-mile visibility and everything was seen in a dun-colored light.

The air was filled with dust. It burned your eyes, and choked your lungs, and gritted between your teeth. And all the while the wind, sweeping across a hundred miles of desert, was gusting at sixty to seventy miles an hour and increasing in intensity. At times, it hit with such force it all but spun you around in your tracks.

Doc Jones joined us.

"We'll have to search for our camp tomorrow!" he said sourly. "Blew away before we could get to it."

He gave us a hand tugging the heavy canvas to the diggings. En route he asked himself a question out loud. "Why'd the storm come at this moment? Why?"

Of course, we Tailboners knew, but, then, we weren't scientifically trained.

"What happened to the camera plates?" I asked, remembering the Graflex film holders containing the newly exposed film of the burials.

"Probably ruined!" Doc Jones answered. "They'd been blown to the ground and covered with sand when I found them. The sand will have scratched the emulsion bare."

We reached the excavated room site to find the precious bones already obliterated from sight by a powdery covering of desert sands.

The canvas tarp was placed on the windward side of the excavation and unfolded. Then we tried to pull the trailing edge over the open digging. It was like trying to hang onto the end of a bull whip. Doc Jones was dumped into the excavation. Toby and I were tossed ten feet away. The tarp jerked loose from the other fellows and took off like an Arabian magic carpet.

Doc Jones poked his head out of the dust filled excavation, coughing and wheezing. "Close your eyes and cover your nose with your handkerchiefs!" he shouted.

We were already hunched over, backs to the wind, trying to keep from being upended—like the tumbleweed and sage rolling over the desert floor, before the wind.

Soon our lungs were so dust filled it seemed impossible that we could survive. Then, as suddenly as it had come, the storm passed.

The air was strangely calm, the wind's roar stilled. The sun continued to shine for a few more minutes before it dipped below the desert's western rim. The desert was a widening expanse of time and space in all directions but the east, where a retreating wall of dust still curtained off a part of our familiar horizon.

We stood up, beating dust from our clothes, brushing it from face and neck and arms.

Darkness came almost as suddenly as had the storm, and with the dark, a roof of twinkling stars appeared. I was lying on my back, gazing heavenward, my mind untroubled, when the coyote howled.

We hadn't heard a coyote all the time we'd been at the site. Now, just like Wipala Wiki had said, the night his ancestor's bones were discovered, the coyote howled.

Toby called over softly. "An unscientific thing is happening, Mike, but I think we've been cursed by a thousand-year-old medicine man."

Of course, Doc Jones disagreed, but we no longer cared if he knew we believed in this Indian superstition.

Next day we found about half of our gear scattered over the desert. Our supply truck brought in enough fresh supplies to get us back on our daily routine.

The day after that we "dusted" out the burial room excavation, once again exposing those bones of Chief Wipala Wiki's very, very angry ancestor. We Tailboners viewed this event with noticeable apprehension.

Doc Jones laughed. "Still worried about the Indian's old superstition?" he asked. "Well, I'll tell you what we'll do—when we knock off tonight, we'll take no chance. We'll cover our burial ground with our tarp. . . ." He paused, remembering we had not recovered the canvas.

"Well, it was a good idea," he added lamely.

"Looks like we might need that canvas or some shelter for the bones of the Chief's ancestor," I said, pointing to the southwest.

This time, it was not a cloud of dust, that poked its angry face over the sawtoothed barren rocks of the Copper Mountains. Now it was rain-laden black clouds. In the distance, you could see the slanted streaks of rain falling to the parched desert. And behind the showers, heavy streaks of lightning ripped apart the low-lying black clouds, revealing only more storm area behind.

"That doesn't look like a gentle storm," observed Toby, almost reproachfully. "The old Hohokam curse really has our number."

Doc Jones sputtered in his exasperation and frustration. "If we only had that canvas," he moaned.

"Will the rain destroy the bones?" I asked.

Doc Jones shook his head. "But that pit might take days to dry out, and we haven't that sort of time," he added sourly.

"Not with wedding bells ringing in a few days," declared Two-Bits.

The sun was still shining as the first showers fell. The cool rain, the clean smell of the washed air, the settling of the dust underfoot, the refreshment of our parched skin, were momentary welcome effects of the shower.

But there was more to come. The sun was lost in the gloomy murk of rain-sodden clouds. Behind the showers we could see the heavy wall of rain advancing, we could feel the moistened breath of the wind. But above all was the thundering, reverberating roar and crash of a tremendous electrical storm.

"We couldn't have a shower," moaned Doc Jones. "Absolutely not! We have to have a cloudburst!"

As if in answer, the deluge struck. There were no raindrops. It was closer to buckets of water pouring over you. In seconds, what had appeared as dry, dusty, sandy desert, barren and parched, could not soak up the downfall fast enough. The whole floor of the desert seemed to be a sheet of water. What had been a dry wash in back of our camp was a torrent, which burst its banks and gouged out new and deeper channels.

There was no need for us to seek shelter. Our tents were downed. We merely anchored them more securely and stood shivering in the rain.

"This is the best bath I've had for weeks," Toby stated between chattering teeth, "but I wish someone would turn on a little warm water. I don't believe it myself, but I'm cold!"

Billy Spears, a startled expression on his face, blurted

out, "Hey, there's a deep, trembling roar sort of, I think, it is. . . ."

Toby laughed. "The poor kid's all mixed up."

Doc Jones held up a silencing hand. Then we all heard the noise, a low, steady roar, like a distant waterfall.

"The river, the dry old Gila River, is flooding under this downpour," Doc Jones announced. "Let's go see it."

Anything was better than standing there shivering.

Sure enough, we found the Gila a raging torrent of a river, roaring in a bold, belligerent manner.

"Wow!" murmured Beans Roberts. "Who'd of believed it of the Gila River, and in Arizona, too!"

Toby nodded. "That's because you're still thinking pre-Hohokam curse," he stated. "Like Wipala Wiki said, we're up against some mighty powerful medicine."

"Bunk!" Doc Jones laughed, "but I sure do wish we could warm up."

Toward morning the rain stopped, but the sun was up before we could warm up and dry out. Doc Jones rode down to the river with our truck driver, and hiked back alone in a few minutes.

"The flood's gone. The river's the same old sandy channel—just a few pools left, and they'll be gone after a few hours of this sun."

"The truck get across?" I asked.

"I'm sure it did," he said. "I came right back. Want to see how our digging looks."

"You can sail boats in it," I answered. "I suppose we could try bailing out the water."

We were getting buckets when the supply-truck driver walked into camp. He was muddy up to his waist and more than a little frightened. He answered our question before we asked it. "Quicksand!" he said. "The truck's sunk in up to the bed and still sinking. I almost couldn't get out."

Doc Jones sat down in despair.

"This isn't an ordinary superstitious curse," Toby pointed out.

But Doc Jones would have none of this nonscientific thinking. He sent Billy Spears and Beans Roberts off to bring help.

As the rest of us were bailing water from our excavation, Doc Jones said, "If there's really an Indian curse it's struck out three times now. That'd be par for the course, wouldn't it?"

"Not at all," Toby said. "I imagine Chief Wiki's ancestor is going to stick right with us until we vamoose."

"Well, what's left for the old spook to conjure up?" asked Doc Jones. "We can't have a fire—nothing to burn. Snow storm seems unlikely, even for his magic powers. Never heard of an earthquake over here, no fault line near us."

"Just don't count yourself safe as long as we're here and that boneyard's uncovered," said Toby, who quite obviously was championing Wipala Wiki's ancient ancestor.

By nightfall Beans and Billy had returned, and two tow trucks had pulled our supply truck out of the quicksand. We'd bailed most of the water from our excavation, and there remained but two days before we broke camp—three days till Doc Jones' wedding. You'd think even a scientific mind like his would have known enough by now to leave that boneyard alone. But not our Doc Jones. His last remark, before turning in for the night, was to be ready for a muddy time of it next day. We were going to clean up the boneyard and get new photographs.

Toby groaned. The Tailboners went to bed and a restless sleep, fearful in the knowledge that an unknown disaster would strike us next day.

There wasn't long to wait on the morrow. Doc Jones came out of his tent scratching arms, back, legs.

"That rain must have brought out mosquitoes from somewhere," he said. "I feel like I'd been eaten alive."

"Let's see," I said. "Straighten up!"

Believe me these were no mosquitoe bites. This scientific hunk of protoplasm was peppered with bright red spots.

"Doc Jones," I said, "you look just like our neighbor's kids last spring when they had chicken pox."

Toby nodded. "You sure do look chicken," he said.

"Can't be!" wailed Doc Jones, "the wedding's day after tomorrow."

The supply truck was sent to town and the driver called the University and they sent out a doctor who said it was chicken pox. He also said that because of our close contact, we'd probably all get chicken pox (if we hadn't had it), and he'd have to quarantine all of us until our epidemic was over.

"How long?" Doc Jones asked.

"Can't say," replied the MD. "I'd guess three or four weeks."

Right then, Doc Jones' temperature shot up to the boiling point, and the MD decided he should be taken to a hospital. Before he was carried away, Doc Jones instructed us to cover the boneyard. "Not because of your Indian Chief's superstition," he added, "but so we can preserve the burials for the time when I can return."

Well, it's mid-September now. Doc Jones had complications and is still in the hospital. We're still in camp and only yesterday had two more cases of chicken pox. But rest assured, we lost no time filling in the boneyard. The bones of Chief Wiki's ancient ancestor are nicely covered.

But out here on the desert with nothing to do, just waiting for our quarantine to be lifted so we can go to school, is a dull existence. That's why, one afternoon, I started writing down our Tailbone Patrol's adventures.

And I'll admit I learned something. When you're a Tailboner you get things done, although you seldom wind up doing things the way you originally had intended. I guess that's where the fun and adventure of belonging to the Tailbone Patrol come in. So, probably we'll go right on working to get out of work, which, when you're a Tailboner, is the magic formula for success.